PRAISE FOR
STREET JOURNAL BESTSELLING AUTHOR
JAN MORAN

### *Seabreeze Inn* and *Coral Cottage* series

"A wonderful story... Will make you feel like the sea breeze is streaming through your hair." – Laura Bradbury, Bestselling Author

"A novel that gives fans of romantic sagas a compelling voice to follow." – *Booklist*

"An entertaining beach read with multi-generational context and humor." – *InD'Tale* Magazine

"Wonderful characters and a sweet story." – Kellie Coates Gilbert, Bestselling Author

"A fun read that grabs you at the start." – Tina Sloan, Author and Award-Winning Actress

"Jan Moran is the queen of the epic romance." —Rebecca Forster, *USA Today* Bestselling Author

"The women are intelligent and strong. At the core is a strong, close-knit family." — Betty's Reviews

### The Chocolatier

"A delicious novel, makes you long for chocolate." – *Ciao Tutti*

"Smoothly written...full of intrigue, love, secrets, and romance." – *Lekker Lezen*

### The Winemakers

"Readers will devour this page-turner as the mystery and passions spin out." – *Library Journal*

"As she did in *Scent of Triumph*, Moran weaves knowledge of wine and winemaking into this intense family drama." – *Booklist*

### The Perfumer: Scent of Triumph

"Heartbreaking, evocative, and inspiring, this book is a powerful journey." – Allison Pataki, *NYT* Bestselling Author of *The Accidental Empress*

"A sweeping saga of one woman's journey through World War II and her unwillingness to give up even when faced with the toughest challenges." — Anita Abriel, Author of *The Light After the War*

"A captivating tale of love, determination and reinvention." — Karen Marin, Givenchy Paris

# BOOKS BY JAN MORAN

## Coral Cottage Series

*Coral Cottage*

*Coral Cafe*

*Coral Holiday*

*Coral Weddings*

*Coral Celebration*

*Coral Memories*

## Summer Beach Series

*Seabreeze Inn*

*Seabreeze Summer*

*Seabreeze Sunset*

*Seabreeze Christmas*

*Seabreeze Wedding*

*Seabreeze Book Club*

*Seabreeze Shores*

*Seabreeze Reunion*

*Seabreeze Honeymoon*

*Seabreeze Gala*

*Seabreeze Library*

## Crown Island Series

*Beach View Lane*

*Sunshine Avenue*

*Orange Blossom Way*

## The Love, California Series

*Flawless*

*Beauty Mark*

*Runway*

*Essence*

*Style*

*Sparkle*

## 20th-Century Historical

*Hepburn's Necklace*

*The Chocolatier*

*The Winemakers: A Novel of Wine and Secrets*

*The Perfumer: Scent of Triumph*

*Life is a Cabernet*

USA TODAY BESTSELLING AUTHOR

# JAN MORAN

# Coral
# MEMORIES

## THE CORAL COTTAGE AT SUMMER BEACH
### BOOK SIX

# CORAL MEMORIES

## CORAL COTTAGE AT SUMMER BEACH SERIES
### BOOK 6

## JAN MORAN

SUNNY PALMS

PRESS

Copyright © 2024 Jan Moran. All Rights Reserved.

All rights reserved under International and Pan-American Copyright Conventions, including the right of reproduction in whole or in part in any form or by any electronic or mechanical means including information storage and retrieval systems, without written permission, except in the case of brief quotations embodied in critical articles and reviews.

Library of Congress Cataloging-in-Publication Data
Moran, Jan.
/ by Jan Moran

ISBN 978-1-64778-231-3 (ebook)
ISBN 978-1-64778-232-0 (paperback)
ISBN 978-1-64778-279-5 (paperback)
ISBN 978-1-64778-233-7 (hardcover)
ISBN 978-1-64778-234-4 (large print)
ISBN 978-1-64778-235-1 (audiobook)

Published by Sunny Palms Press. Cover design by Sleepy Fox Studios. Cover images copyright Deposit Photos.

Sunny Palms Press
9663 Santa Monica Blvd STE 1158
Beverly Hills, CA 90210 USA
www.JanMoran.com

# PROLOGUE

Ginger opened the old photo album on the coffee table. Embossed with worn gold lettering, the cover read, *Our Memories.*

Settling against the brocade settee in her airy bedroom overlooking the ocean, she swept back the sleeve of the silk caftan she'd had made in Paris. Like her, it was considered vintage, though the fabric with its violet hues was still as lustrous as the day she'd discovered it. She aimed for her mind to remain just as vibrant, even as her limbs showed signs of age.

Signs of a life well lived, in her opinion.

Her husband's words sprang to mind. *As long as we're living, we should live well.*

To which she'd added—*and find happiness wherever we are.*

She still missed Bertrand, yet his presence remained evident in their private quarters. He had taught her how to live well, regardless of a person's station in life. *The right partner, good friends, a sense of style, and doing what you love.*

She drew a deep breath at the memory. To this day, she kept bottles of his favorite colognes on her dresser. He wore Spanish lavender in the morning and a smoky, spiced sandalwood *parfum* in the evening. The scent on a linen handkerchief he might offer her if needed was lodged in her olfactory cortex.

She smiled at the memory of his sweet gestures. No one could ever replace him. While she'd loved her grand, life-long romance, she was satisfied with her life now.

His last words—passionate yet tinged with humor—floated to her as if through the ether. *Never say never, darling.*

"You rascal," she replied, pursing her lips with a smile. As long as she was still in a relationship with the love of her life, how could she?

Ginger touched the curled edge of a sepia-toned photograph of her parents and siblings. They were frolicking on a beach not far from that which stretched beyond her cottage window. A frothy high tide crashed along the shoreline, conjuring a vivid image of that distant day at the beach.

Footsteps sounded behind her, and her eldest granddaughter joined her. "What did you want to show me?"

Ginger gestured to the photographs. "I don't know if you've ever seen these."

Marina looked at her with a hint of curiosity in her eyes. She peered at the images. "That's a wonderful photo. Do you remember that day?"

"As if it were yesterday, darling." Surely Marina didn't think she was waning just yet. Ginger lifted an eyebrow in mild reproach, yet her granddaughter's gaze held such keen interest she realized that was only Marina's way of asking for the story behind the photograph.

Perhaps it was time her granddaughters learned about her past. They needed to know why she'd told the stories she had—before her history was lost forever.

Anything could happen at any time.

Like that day Bertrand had left their suite at the Ritz for an afternoon swim before dressing for dinner.

Ginger blinked back the memory. *There were so many things I wish I'd asked him.*

Marina shifted the heavy photo album toward her lap, sharing its weight. "I recognize your parents. Who are the others in that photo?"

"My brother Jesse and our friends." Ginger named everyone and added a little backstory on each of them.

Yet, she hardly knew where to begin in telling her own story. Over the years, she had woven many tales for her granddaughters. While she grieved the tragedy of her only child, Sandi, and her husband, Dennis, she also bore the responsibility of their three daughters left behind. Without Bertrand, she'd had no choice but to carry on.

Life had a way of laughing at the plans one made.

Afterward, she guided and protected the girls with every sliver of determination and creativity she could muster. Her girls had grown into lovely, accomplished women with their own families. She was proud of every Delavie descendant.

Ginger had been the matriarch of her family for decades, having outlived her two older brothers by many years. One was lost in a distant war, another from an ailment that could have been treated today. Someday, one of her granddaughters—all young women now—would inherit her title of matriarch. That would be Marina if the natural order of life prevailed.

Not that it did, she knew, coughing and surreptitiously touching the polished coffee table for luck.

Marina looked concerned. "Would you like a glass of water?"

"That would be lovely. Thank you, dear."

The nagging thought arose again. *My granddaughters should know their family history.*

Marina brought a glass of water to her and settled beside her as Ginger sipped it. She glanced at another image. "Are those your brothers?"

Returning her focus to the old photographs, Ginger let out a small sigh of remembrance. "Yes, the four of us. We were nearly inseparable then." She glanced at Marina. "Tell me, how is Jack? Is he busy?"

Marina looked mildly surprised at the change of subject. "He just finished an assignment. Until edits from your publisher are returned, he plans to sift through ideas for another project and spend time with Leo."

Ginger nodded thoughtfully. She may have a window of opportunity. Marina's husband, Jack, had won awards for his work in investigative journalism. Since they had been collaborating on a successful series of children's books, she had grown to trust him.

Jack had been angling to write her biography for some time.

With her memory still excellent, Ginger recalled everything. She turned the page and pointed to a photo of her younger brother, who remained forever young in her mind. "This was Jesse."

She was acutely aware of the passage of time. Even

now, she felt her brother's presence, as she always had. His memory still motivated her.

In essence, she was determined to live for both of them. Ginger had learned to listen to her intuition, and now she wondered at the sudden urge to memorialize her life. "I should make notes about the family."

Gently, Marina touched her shoulder. "I'd like that. Brooke and Heather would, too. And Jack thinks you've led such a fascinating life."

"I've been fortunate," Ginger replied, shrugging off her granddaughter's admiration.

"You've always told us that we create our luck," Marina said. "Do you think you've done that in your life?"

"Luck cuts both ways, my dear." Yet, besides her resolve, Ginger considered herself born lucky—even destined. "Some fortune is earned; some is a pure gift."

Her great fortune was in her brain's natural processing power, pattern recognition, neuroplasticity, and nearly total memory recall. Even as a child, she'd experienced the world in mathematical terms. Patterns, such as the Fibonacci sequence—and many others—shimmered to her consciousness in countless areas, from nature and stock market charts to the codes she enjoyed disassembling.

As much as she had worked to illuminate the truth, she had also been required to conceal it.

Ginger turned the page to her wedding photos and pressed a hand to her heart. *This photo...we had such a wonderful life ahead of us then.* A few short years later, she would discover more riveting pursuits for her skills.

Marina leaned in. "Grandpa looked like a movie star."

"Even better, in my mind." Warmth filled her chest. Her Bertrand was incredibly handsome.

Marina studied the old photo. "You were very young when you married."

"You weren't but a few years older."

Marina nodded in acknowledgment. "Still, I can't imagine Heather being married. She and Blake seem serious, but I want her to get to know him better."

Ginger had married for love, though she likely would have followed a different path today. At that time, few positions for women with keen mathematical abilities existed. Rather than wither under endless, meaningless conversations with boys her age, she'd chosen life with a more exciting man of thirty.

"Was it love at first sight between you and Grandpa?" Marina asked.

"I don't believe in insta-love." Ginger sniffed. "Still, I quickly deduced that Bertrand and I were an excellent fit, and I wasn't wrong. He became the love of my life."

She had grown to love him much more than the day they married. Bertrand saw her as she truly was. He admired her intelligence and encouraged her; her success didn't dim his in any way.

Her sweet darling Sandi was born the following year.

The old wound in her heart opened once again, but Ginger caught herself. Years ago, she'd sworn to remember Sandi with joy rather than grief. With a slight lift of her chin, Ginger regained her smile. How fortunate that she had a trio of lovely granddaughters.

Marina scanned the photos. "And this ship?"

"That was our maiden voyage to France. Oh, what a

world we stepped into." Even today, her skin tingled with the anticipation she'd felt. She would never forget the grand ball in Paris that changed her life—or anything that happened afterward.

Especially what happened afterward.

Her youngest granddaughter Kai swept into the room, her sunflower print sundress swirling around her. "A letter just arrived for you, Ginger. It's handwritten, so I thought it might be important."

"All letters were once handwritten," Ginger said with a smile of amusement. She took the letter and instantly recognized the sender's name.

"Who is Oliver Powell?" Kai asked, leaning over her shoulder.

Marina shot her an annoyed look. "Give her some privacy."

"What, like it's her boyfriend?"

Ginger chuckled at the thought. "No, darlings. Kurt Powell was my first boss. Oliver was his younger brother whom I met years later when Bertrand and I visited New York. He was closer to my age. Quite a charmer in his day."

"So, open it," Kai said, handing her a brass letter opener from her desk.

Ginger stared at the letter, dreading the contents. Kurt and Bertrand were old schoolmates. He would be in his ninth decade now. She sliced the envelope and removed the letter.

*Dearest Ginger, I write this with a heavy heart. My dear brother Kurt has moved on from this realm.*

She nodded sadly. "As I expected," she said, folding the letter to read later.

"He says they're having a celebration of life ceremony in Laguna Beach," Kai said. "Isn't that like a party?"

"It's a celebration of one's life," Ginger replied. "Would you put that on my nightstand?"

Kai unfolded the letter. "He's invited you, so you should go."

"Don't be so nosy," Marina said.

"I'm only reading the interesting parts." Kai brightened. "If you don't want to go alone, I'll go with you."

"There will likely be many old friends there," Ginger said. It wouldn't be the same without Bertrand, though. Why, the fun they'd once had. *Oliver Powell.* She smiled, recalling how they used to go out with him and his wife.

Marina shot her sister another look. "Come sit with us. Ginger has some old family photos for us to see. Someday, you'll be showing these to your little one."

"If she ever arrives." Kai plopped down on the other side of her grandmother.

Ginger turned the page. Jack had been angling to write her story since they'd met. While she intended to share everything with him, a question nagged at her.

Was it time to write her life story, or did she have adventures yet to live?

# 1

Marina peered through the door to the sunroom in their beach cottage. Jack sat in front of a large-screen computer with headphones clamped over his ears. She inched closer, curious what he was working on, though trying not to be intrusive.

Her husband didn't like to share his work until he was ready. He'd once told her, *No one wants to see a writer's first draft.* She could understand that.

She made out her grandmother's name on the screen. Suddenly, the sun slid from behind a cloud, casting her shadow over the monitor's screen.

"What the—" Jack jerked off his headphones and whirled around, his thick, unruly hair sticking up. He exhaled in relief when he saw her. "I thought you'd left."

"Forgot my phone. I'm sorry I crept up on you." Given his former career as a reporter who frequently worked on explosive stories, he could still be on edge. "Is that a new book?"

Letting out a sigh of relief, he waved to the screen. "I'm making notes about things Ginger says before I forget. She had a couple of zingers the other day."

She smoothed a hand over his shoulder. "We call those Gingerisms. They're unique."

"I've been trying to piece together a narrative, but her memory shifts." He pinched the bridge of his nose with concern. "Do you think she might be…"

"Growing senile?" Marina smiled and shook her head at her grandmother's harmless deceptions. "Her recollections have been changing for decades. My sisters thought she was embellishing stories and simply forgot how she'd told them before. But I don't think that was it. She has nearly total recall of anything important. Or trivial."

Jack pulled her onto his lap and nuzzled her neck. "Then why the variation in her recollections?"

"I think she's simply entertaining us." Another thought occurred to Marina. "But given Bertrand's diplomatic career—and her work that we've discovered—she might have been protecting us. Or others. You'll have to ask her sometime."

"What if I uncover something you don't want to know about?"

"I doubt you'll find anything nefarious in her past."

Jack had been interested in writing a book about Ginger for a long time. Yet, when Marina had first learned about it before they married, she was furious. Now, she was glad Jack was making notes. As for Ginger's biography, Marina still wasn't sure if it was a good idea.

Marina sensed that Ginger had secrets, even if she

never said that. When her grandmother wanted to avoid questions, she could have an airy, glib manner. If people didn't know Ginger like she and her sisters did, they wouldn't think anything of it.

Marina had interviewed enough people when reporting the news in San Francisco to learn body language and detect when a subject wasn't telling the entire truth.

Yet, her grandmother was an expert at concealment; she'd give her that. Marina probably would have missed the clues if she hadn't been a professional.

Jack tapped a search tab on his screen. "Did Ginger ever mention crediting her accomplishments to others?"

"That might have happened, especially when she was working with men." Marina thumped his shoulder.

"Hey, I always give credit."

"I know you do. I'm talking about back then. The norms were different."

Marina and Kai had recently discovered praise for their grandmother's work as a cryptologist in old articles online. They'd been surprised, because they knew her as a statistician and math teacher. They thought she loved puzzles, ciphers, and codes simply as hobbies.

That was the way her interest began, Marina suspected. However, it went far beyond that.

Jack leaned in for a kiss, and she relished the touch of his lips.

He groaned with pleasure. "Why don't you call in sick to the cafe? With the kids out of the house..."

She smiled against his lips. "Hold that thought until later." A private party had booked her Coral Cafe for an early brunch before the lunch run. She pushed herself from his lap and sashayed out.

Jack chuckled and whistled after her.

Their new marriage was off to a good start. She adored Jack's son Leo, who would be in middle school next year. Her daughter Heather was living with Ginger in the home she'd had for decades, right next to the cafe. Marina liked being close enough to her grandmother to check on her.

Still, Ginger was nearly as active as she'd always been, even in her eighties. She hiked, practiced yoga, and danced like someone half her age. As for her intellectual stamina, she grew more astute and formidable with age.

HOURS LATER, after the brunch party and a busy lunch run, the crowd at the Coral Cafe had thinned. Only a handful of guests still lingered at tables.

Marina turned to her sous chef. "Cruise, would you take over from here, please."

The young man with the tattoos and bleached hair wound into a man-bun nodded. "Got it, Chef. Any news on that other food truck?"

"I haven't heard from the loan officer yet. Shouldn't be much longer, though. I'll return later to help with that catering job."

"You don't have to," Cruise said, grinning. "We've got this."

She nodded her approval. "Glad to hear it. Please call me when Kai arrives." They were planning a video shoot today.

"Sure thing. I'll clean up the place."

Cruise oversaw the team she'd trained on the Coral Cafe food truck, which had grown to produce significant revenue. Besides its daytime route, the truck was also booked nearly every weekend for parties and beach weddings.

Marina's catering business had grown, too. She could breathe easier now that her business had earned plenty of repeat customers and a reputation for excellence. She no longer had to worry about meeting payroll every month. Another food truck would build her business in beach communities south of Summer Beach.

She would have plenty of time to work on that later. For now, the conversations she'd had with Ginger and Jack lingered in her mind.

Her grandmother had casually asked if Jack was busy. Yet, Ginger seldom made small talk without aim.

And Jack still had a keen desire to write her grandmother's story, whatever that might entail.

A thought occurred to Marina. She might find more family history in her grandfather's study. He'd also been a force in his lifetime.

Marina glanced at the clock. She had some time before their shoot.

After crossing the short distance from the cafe to Ginger's cottage, Marina made her way into the study. She opened the door, greeted by the sweet scent of aged pipe tobacco that had permeated the pages of every book and lingered in the air.

She glanced at the yellow manila folders still in his desk

drawer but didn't see anything unusual. At the built-in bookcase, she ran her fingers across the books Bertrand Delavie had written on leadership and diplomacy. Yet, the more stories Marina pieced together, the more she realized that Ginger also had a compelling story.

How many women could say they had once been cryptologists or contributed to the course of history?

Marina wished she knew more of what Ginger had worked on. When asked questions about her past, her grandmother could be vague. Another thought occurred to her. Over the years, Ginger often took trips with friends, though Marina and her sisters had never met them.

Did those people even exist?

Or was Marina imagining things now?

She slid a book from the shelf and opened it. Dust particles rose from yellowed pages brittle with age. She flipped to the back of the book and searched the sources. An author of an article about probabilities jumped out at her.

G.E. Delavie.

Although everyone called her grandmother Ginger, her given name was Grace Ellen. She was born with ginger-colored hair, so the nickname stuck—even among her grandchildren. Marina smiled to herself. She was the one who'd cast aside the grandmother title and called her Ginger like Grandpa did.

Precocious, some probably thought, but what did she know at that age?

Marina reviewed the attribution. Had Ginger written this article, or was this a coincidence? She would research this later.

Her sister Kai appeared in the doorway, a vision in a flowing floral sundress, a lightweight sweater looped around her shoulders, and a large bag on her arm. "Hey, you. Cruise said you'd gone this way. Ready for our filming?"

"You're early for a change. I just needed a break."

Kai sauntered toward her. "So you decided to spend it here looking at dusty old books when you have a sunny beach a few steps away?"

"I've been thinking about all Ginger has done in her life." She showed her sister the book she was looking at. "Check this out. *G. E. Delavie.*"

"Is that a relative?"

"I think it's Ginger. Her name is Grace Ellen, remember? I'm going to ask her about that article."

Kai smoothed a hand over her rounded abdomen in thought. "She's always downplayed her accomplishments."

"Yet she's always been confident about her abilities." One of their grandmother's favorite sayings was, *Let's get on with it.* To her, there was always another mountain to climb, another goal to reach and surpass. Marina suspected her impacts had likely been more significant than any of them knew.

Marina watched Kai's motions. "How's the baby today?"

"Practicing kickboxing," she replied. "Brooke's baby is chill, but this one has plenty of energy. I'll have to stay in shape to keep up with it."

Marina grinned, thinking of when she was pregnant with her twins. Her younger sisters were expecting their babies only a few weeks apart—Kai with her first and Brooke with her fourth.

Leaning against the desk, Marina asked, "Remember that article we saw online? It talked about how Ginger had trained and inspired other women in that Cold War code-breaking outfit. People have made movies about that kind of work."

"Maybe now is the time to talk to her. What about Jack? He always wanted to write her story."

Marina grew quiet for a moment. "Any book Jack writes is bound to get a lot of attention. How do you think she'd feel about that now?"

Kai wrinkled her nose. "After embellishing her stories for years, she might not remember the real version."

"I think she's still plenty sharp."

Yet, their grandmother wasn't getting any younger, even though Ginger enjoyed exceptional health for her age. Her brisk walks on the beach and vigorous hikes to her favorite meditation spot on the ridgetop kept her in shape. Her incredible will drove her every day.

Kai reached out and shut the book in Marina's hands. "That will be there tomorrow. Let's start the video shoot while the cafe is slow. Besides, you need hair and makeup."

"You told me to look natural." Marina smoothed a hand over her wispy hair.

Kai arched an eyebrow. "You look like you've been working in a hot kitchen."

"That's because I have been."

"I'm not letting you on camera like that. You should know better."

Marina nudged her sister. "Work your magic, then."

She followed Kai to the spacious hall bathroom of the

old cottage. While Kai opened the bag she carried, Marina settled into a chair in front of the mirror. "I don't want to look theatrical. I want to look like I do every day at the cafe."

Kai opened her makeup bag, a glint of excitement in her eyes. "You'll look that way on camera, I promise. Only better."

Her sister hummed a Broadway tune as she worked. Marina guessed it was a song from *West Side Story* that Kai had once performed.

Kai cleansed her face and applied foundation to minimize the sheen, much as Marina had done for her on-camera work on the morning news in San Francisco, which seemed another lifetime ago.

"Hey, you look great," Brooke said as she joined them. Her hair was in braids, and her sun-kissed face from gardening didn't need makeup, although she had applied lipstick. "We're all ready to go."

Ginger was behind her, looking casually elegant in her pressed coral shirt and pearls. "What a wonderful idea this is," she said, clasping her hands. "Three generations of the Delavie family cooking together."

"Thank you all for being a part of this," Marina said. "The Coral Cafe wouldn't exist without you."

Her daughter Heather had already dressed and was gathering the chef jackets and aprons they would use for the shoot. This video was Kai's idea. Marina would use it for publicity and the Coral Cafe website.

After Kai finished, they made their way to the cafe. A lighting technician from Kai and Axe's outdoor amphitheater was already there, lighting the space with the necessary brightness.

Kai brought out several tripods designed for phones and began to set them up. "Marina, I need your phone. Brooke and Heather, yours, too."

Marina looked on with interest. "What are you doing?"

"I picked up tips and techniques when we filmed routines for promotional pieces on my last tour," Kai replied. "I watched what the camera operators and the director were doing. When I edit this piece, I can pull different camera angles. I'm also filming vertical clips for social media. That's what we do for our stage productions. It's easy on the budget, and we adjust everything in post-production."

Behind them, Cruise finished wiping down the stove. "I'll get out of your way, ladies."

Kai held up a hand. "Not so fast. I'll want a few shots of you, too. You're the food truck chef." She twisted her lips to one side and opened her makeup bag. "Men need powder, too. Heather, would you take care of that while I set up the shots?"

Cruise grinned while Heather whisked a brush across his nose and cheeks. Then, the two of them posed for Kai.

After Kai finished the shots, she turned to Cruise. "I'll need your help with filming," she added, adjusting the settings.

Marina looked doubtful. "Are you sure these small devices can produce a good video?"

"As long as you know what you're doing and have good lighting," Kai replied.

Marina relaxed. After finishing a season at the outdoor

amphitheater she ran with Axe, Kai was an experienced director with a good eye now.

While they waited, Cruise twirled Heather around, and she laughed. Quickly, Kai caught it on video. "Love the energy. Keep it up, everyone."

Marina was pleased that she'd brought Cruise back on board after their disagreement earlier in the year. Their working relationship had improved. He listened to her and followed directions now, and she worked with him on new dishes and recipes, drawing on his training in top hotel kitchens.

Together, they developed a new food truck menu featuring specialty items and standards that could be prepared quickly in the small space. These included gourmet hamburgers with sweet potato fries, fish tacos with crunchy vegetables, and shrimp pizza with pesto sauce.

Kai turned to Marina. "Now, I need a few shots of you and Ginger."

Marina posed with Ginger in the kitchen, and Kai snapped photos from different angles.

"All right, we're ready to record." Kai showed Cruise what to do.

"Welcome to the Coral Cafe," Marina began. "I'm Marina Moore, and I'm here with three generations of my family." She went on to introduce Ginger, Brooke, and Heather.

She and Kai had written a script for the dish they were preparing, a simple salad made with seasonal fruits and vegetables.

"Many of our most popular dishes are based on old family recipes that my grandmother Ginger Delavie developed." Marina gestured to Brooke, who held a bountiful basket of fresh vegetables. "My sister Brooke is an organic gardener. Besides finding her fresh produce at the Summer Beach farmers market, you can also find it in many of our most popular dishes, such as this one."

She paused and gestured to Heather as she introduced her. "My daughter serves in the cafe, or you might see her on our food truck at special events."

"And cut," Kai said, gesturing. "You're off to a good start. Now let's get cooking."

"Just in time," Brooke said, laughing. "I need a break, and I bet you do, too, Kai."

"Two pregnant women in the family is a double blessing," Ginger said, smiling. "We'll take frequent breaks for you."

Marina knew their grandmother was thrilled with the new additions to the family—they all were—and it almost made Marina wish for a child with Jack.

Almost, that is. Her twins were grown, and Jack had Leo to look after.

Their family was expanding in Summer Beach. Only her son Ethan was missing, though he visited when he could. He'd been playing in amateur golf tournaments the last few months and had won a few. He was following his dream of turning pro and getting close.

When her sisters returned, Kai and Brooke were in good spirits, with Brooke laughing over her predicament. With three rowdy boys at home, she and her husband hadn't planned to have another child. On the other hand, Kai and her husband Axe tried to start a family for some time, and Kai worried they might not have any luck.

Just then, a smaller version of Jack tore around the corner, with Jack following close behind.

Marina threw an arm around Leo. "Did you come to watch us film the video?"

Leo grinned with excitement. "Dad said I can, as long as I'm quiet."

"Hope that's okay." Jack pressed a kiss to Marina's cheek. "Don't want to mess up your lipstick."

"I'll risk it," she said, stealing a kiss.

"Hey, you two," Kai said. "Knock it off. I don't have another makeup artist here."

"Get this on film, will you?" Grinning, Jack swooped Marina into a deep dip, and she exploded with laughter.

"Got it," Kai said, chuckling. "Places, everyone," she called out, and the family scrambled back to their marks. "We're rolling on three, two, and one." She pointed, and they began.

As Marina began preparing a summer salad with avocados, cucumbers, and red and yellow cherry tomatoes, she stayed with the script, but Ginger and Brooke quickly veered from it.

Kai motioned for them to keep going, so Marina ad-libbed, and soon they were working together as they always did in the kitchen. Along the way, they laughed and made a couple of blunders. Brooke washed and trimmed the produce while Heather brought out supplies. Ginger's quick wit and Marina's knife skills brought the ingredients together in a colorful dish they served in Mexican Talavera bowls.

"And that's a wrap," Kai said, shooting a look at Cruise.

"We should do it over," Marina said. "Maybe we laughed too much?"

"And one of the cucumbers got away from me," Brooke added, bending to pick it up from the floor.

Kai waved a hand. "I'll take care of that in editing. I can work with what we have."

"Then let's pour the champagne and fizzy apple juice," Ginger said, clapping.

They all gathered in the kitchen, celebrating with a toast.

Marina held up her glass. "To Ginger, for showing us all how to believe in our dreams."

"The Coral Cafe is proof of that," Ginger added, tapping glasses and trading embraces. "You improved my recipes and added your own."

Heather leaned against the kitchen counter. "Mom, you should write a cookbook, like Martha Stewart or Giada De Laurentiis."

Ginger's eyes lit. "Why, what a marvelous idea."

"Do you think people need another cookbook?" Marina wasn't so sure.

"You've won awards for your fancy seafood pizza," Heather replied. "People often ask for recipes at the cafe. If you create a cookbook, I know I could sell it for you."

"I'll think about that." With the growth of her business, Marina recorded her recipes to share with her expanding team. The idea of writing a cookbook appealed to her. It could be a good marketing tool—and pay for Heather's final year of tuition if they did it right. "As long as I have help putting it together."

"If you give me your recipes, I can write a first draft."

Heather's eyes sparkled. "Let's talk later. Blake is picking me up soon."

"Tell him hello for me." Marina liked the young man her daughter had been dating.

Brooke turned to Kai, who was still standing by the tripods. "Come join us."

"In a minute." Kai's eyes shimmered with happiness. "Another break and I'll be there. Brooke, pour a glass of the bubbly apple juice for me."

Ginger turned to Jack and handed him a glass of champagne. "Do join us. You're family, too." When he accepted the glass, Ginger peered at him. "Sounds like you're going to have another writer in the family," she said, nodding toward Marina.

"You might have to help me, too," Marina said to Ginger.

"I'd like that." Ginger inclined her head. "In fact, I have another book in mind."

Jack touched her glass with his and sipped his champagne. "For our children's book series?"

"No, not that." Ginger peered at him over the rim of her glass, apprising his reaction. "You've been wanting to write my story."

Jack coughed in mid-sip, sputtering his reply. "Uh, yes, ma'am. You're serious?"

"We're well past the *ma'am* phase, Jack." Ginger lifted her chin. "And yes, I'm quite serious. It's time I began recording my memories for all of you."

Marina looked concerned at Ginger and reached for Jack's hand. She wondered what had precipitated this change of heart on her grandmother's part. Ginger had been feeling nostalgic lately, sharing photos and memories with her.

Was she feeling well?

The thought of anything happening to her grandmother filled Marina with anxiety. She still needed Ginger.

They all did.

## 2

*T*he late afternoon sun filtered through the windows of Ginger's cottage, casting delicate shadows across her antique Balinese writing desk. She was sorting through old photographs for her meeting with Jack when her phone rang, breaking the silence.

"Hello?" she answered, curious about the unfamiliar number.

"Ginger Delavie? It's Oliver Powell. Kurt's brother."

She smiled as memories flooded back. "Why, what a lovely surprise. I've thought of you so often. How are you, dear?"

"I'm doing alright, considering everything," he replied. "I wondered if you received the invitation to Kurt's celebration of life in Laguna Beach?"

"Yes, I did." Ginger softened her tone. "I would be delighted to attend. Kurt held a special place in my life, and he was like a brother to Bertrand."

"They were practically inseparable throughout school

and later at Harvard. It was like I had two older brothers, especially after Bertrand's parents passed away."

"And how is Margaret?"

There was a brief pause before Oliver continued, "I'm a widower now, Ginger. Margaret passed two years ago."

"Oh, I'm so sorry, Oliver." Ginger pressed a hand to her chest, feeling the pain of that loss. "I didn't know."

"It's okay. You knew how Margaret was; she didn't want any fuss. We had a small ceremony for our family. It comforts me to know she's in a good place now."

Ginger remembered Margaret. She had been quiet and introverted, though she was a sweet woman dedicated to her loved ones.

"How are you managing?" she asked, her heart aching for him.

"I'm much better now. Thanks for asking."

They fell into an easy conversation, catching up on old friends and their paths since they'd last seen each other at Bertrand's funeral. Ginger laughed at Oliver's witty observations and felt a warmth she hadn't experienced in years.

When there was a lull in the conversation, Oliver asked, "Did you ever remarry after Bertrand?"

"No, I never tried to replace him," she replied. "There are few men like Bertrand."

"I agree," Oliver said. "He always said that life should be lived to the fullest. Maybe we shouldn't close ourselves off to new possibilities."

Curious now, she had to ask. "Have you been seeing anyone?"

"No, but I'm open to surprises," he replied with a small chuckle.

His words resonated with her, stirring something long forgotten in her. "Life certainly has a way of doing that."

Ginger enjoyed talking to him. His intelligence and humor were refreshing, and their shared history gave them a great deal in common to talk about.

"I shouldn't monopolize your time," he finally said. "I wanted to talk to you before the event and remind you not to wear black. This event is a fond celebration, not a funeral. That's how Kurt wanted it. He told me he wanted to look down on one last festive event."

"That sounds like Kurt. He was always the life of the party."

Oliver cleared his throat on a husky note. "I look forward to seeing you soon."

"As do I, Oliver," she replied. Then, surprising herself, she added, "Feel free to call if you need help with anything." A smile played on her lips as she hung up the phone.

Ginger sat back in her chair, recalling their past friendship with fondness. She checked her calendar and marked the date of Oliver's event for Kurt. She would attend, she decided.

JACK ARRIVED SHORTLY after she hung up with Oliver. She answered the door with a stack of old photos in her hand.

"Visuals will help you imagine what my world was like," Ginger said as she welcomed him. "Come with me. I've been sorting things on the dining room table."

"Sure will. I appreciate that." Jack surveyed the stack of papers and photo albums on the wooden table.

"Have a seat." She had prepared for this meeting with a pot of his favorite Earl Grey tea, a pad of yellow sticky notes, and copies of articles she'd written years ago.

Jack slid out a chair for her before taking a seat. She smiled at his manners, pleased that Marina had chosen a partner well this time—not that Stan hadn't been a prince of a man, too. But that Grady—what he had done to Marina still irked her. Yet, if her fiancé hadn't acted in such a dreadful way, Marina wouldn't have fled to Summer Beach or met Jack. Ginger loved having Marina nearby, along with her bustling cafe.

"You're the wordsmith," Ginger began, pouring tea for Jack. She noticed him watching her with respect. "I've always been driven by ideas and possibilities. Of right and wrong—although the world operates in shades of gray, I've discovered."

"Thank you," Jack said, accepting the tea. "Before we begin, I'm curious. Your biography—why now?"

"Is that Marina's inquiry or yours?"

"Fair enough. She voiced the question, although I wondered, too."

"First of all, you're available. To find talent such as yourself, with your credentials, in Summer Beach is rare." Avoiding questions of age, illness, or mortality, she added, "The time simply seemed right."

Jack nodded at this explanation. He opened a notebook and clicked a pen. "I know you well enough to flesh out the foundational material, so we can skip those questions. The stories we share reveal our outlook, life experiences, and subsequent learnings. We're hard-wired for stories, especially those that humanize the subject. That's where we can start."

"Well, I am very much a human," Ginger said. "Must we establish that?"

Jack's face colored. "What I meant was—"

"I'm only teasing you, my dear," Ginger said, opening the album she had shared with Marina. "Let's begin with my family history. Early childhood shapes us, don't you think? Then, as adults, we must decide to continue on our parents' path or change our journey."

Nodding, Jack made a note. "Can you be more specific?"

"Of course."

Jack waited for her to elaborate, but her mind was racing ahead, connecting the dots, the cause and effect of myriad choices—some small, some momentous.

She tapped a photo, naming her family members. "My parents met in Oklahoma and moved west. This photo was taken just before my brother Calvin left for university. I was excited at the thought I would soon join him."

"And did you?"

That question made her hesitate. A memory flooded her mind, and the years slipped away.

"No, I'm afraid not."

"Surely you showed great promise in those subjects as a child."

"True, but…"

Leaning forward, Jack pressed on, his voice soft with empathy. "You must have been disappointed. I'd sure like to hear that story."

"Well, alright." As she began telling her story, she felt like she was there again.

---

SEATED at a second-hand dining room table scarred from use, Ginger closed her schoolbooks. She'd finished early today.

In the adjoining living room of the small cottage, the rhythmic sound of sewing shears slicing through cotton fabric broke the silence. Her mother worked at a padded cutting table that folded out from the wall.

The aroma of tea filled the air. It was too warm outside for hot tea, so Mary Lou Sheraton often let it grow cold before drinking. Cut fabric panels stacked nearby would be dresses come morning.

Ginger often slept to the sound of her mother pumping the foot treadle of her sewing machine, its needle piercing the fabric.

She stuffed her homework into her book bag for school tomorrow. She had just enough time to swim before helping her mother prepare dinner. Her gingham dress was scratchy and damp with perspiration. She stood, ready to bolt. "May I go to the beach with my friends now? Their parents will watch us."

Her mother shook her head. "Not today. Calvin and Buford need help with their homework."

"They never help me."

The scissors fell silent. "Grace Ellen, watch your mouth."

Ginger tried to look remorseful, but she was tired of

carrying the homework load for her brothers. "Mama, they must learn calculus and trigonometry for their exams."

"That is precisely why they need your help now," her mother replied patiently. "Calvin must pass if he is to graduate from high school. You have a natural aptitude for this material, so share your blessings with your brothers. To do otherwise would be selfish."

"But I haven't taken those classes yet." She would have, except one teacher blocked her request and insisted home economics was a prudent alternative.

Her mother arched an eyebrow. "You've read those books cover to cover and earned credit for the classes, thanks to Miss Carter and the principal." She put down her scissors and picked up her teacup. "When you're older, you'll be glad you helped your brothers."

"Mama, I know what I want to do." Ginger had been waiting for the right time to share her dream with her mother. If she couldn't go to the beach, she'd make her pitch before her father came home.

Her mother would understand.

Ginger placed her bag near the door. "I just learned today that Scott is graduating early with a university scholarship. My grades are better than his. Except in home economics." Ginger made a face.

"Nothing wrong with being a fine cook." Her mother peered over the rim of her cup. "And your grades are the best in the school." Pride filled her voice.

"Then let me apply to the university like Scott did," Ginger pleaded. "My teachers will support me, and I've challenged and received credit for every math class offered. I'm so far ahead I'm bored. I don't want to wait to study the advanced math I'll need for a degree in engineering."

Her mother looked out the window toward the ocean and its relentless waves. Slowly, she dragged her gaze back to her daughter. "You want so much, honey."

Feeling confused, Ginger stared at her. Her mother had supported her dreams in the past; why wouldn't she now? "Please, let me try."

"You take after my father, dear." Her mother shook her head. "He was such a brilliant man."

The rear door slammed, startling her mother. She stashed her supplies and folded the table away. "He's home early. Go help your brothers, and I'll start dinner."

A wave of panic swept over Ginger. "This is my chance; I know it. I could go to school with Calvin and Scott."

Her father entered the room, the smell of the sea and his fishing vessel clinging to his clothes. "Your chance for what, Ginger?"

Quickly, she told him about her plan. "I could leave home with Calvin and continue with him. I know I can do this. I can solve problems others can't."

Her father gazed at her with a mixture of pity and pride. "I'll bet you can, peanut. You're one heck of a chess player. At least I can still win against your brothers."

"Give me a chance, Pa. Please."

He rubbed the stubble on his chin and frowned at her mother. "That's not for you."

Ginger was stunned at his words. "But, Pa, it's perfect for me. There will be people I can finally relate to who'll understand me. I can study engineering—"

"A lady engineer, imagine that!" He chuckled. "You need to be reasonable. Education requires a lot of money."

"My teachers think I can get scholarships."

"You will finish high school," her father replied, his stern tone indicating the conversation was over. He turned to leave, shower, and change his clothes, just as he did six days a week.

Sensing her time was running out, Ginger seized the chance to clarify his mandate. "Once I graduate from high school, then I can go?"

Her father glanced at her mother, and another guarded look passed between them. "Mary Lou, haven't you discussed this with your daughter?"

"But she's so talented." Her mother lifted her shoulders and let them fall—a familiar signal of helplessness against her husband's decisions.

Ginger knew that was an act. Her mother was intelligent, even though she hadn't finished school because every hand was needed on the farm.

It didn't matter in the end. They were among many families who lost their homesteads and moved west in search of work and opportunities. Her father, proud as he was, was forced to let his wife work to put food on the table.

Mary Lou was an excellent seamstress, and she had taken in sewing for years. After settling in Summer Beach, which was then barely a town, they clawed their way back from financial ruin to a moderately comfortable station in life. Her father still bore the scars.

Watching her mother, Ginger set her jaw. Mary Lou Sheraton often minimized her intelligence in her husband's presence, deferring decisions to him.

Ginger would never do that. Her favorite teacher at school—Beatrice Carter, who'd worked as a machinist at a factory in nearby Long Beach during the Second World War—told her women had more opportunities than ever now.

After hearing that, Ginger had decided she wouldn't marry for a while. First, she would get an education, have an exciting career, and travel the world.

She stepped toward her father. She'd grown as tall as he was in the last two years. Ginger angled her chin at him. "If Scott can go to university a year early—"

"Scott Smithson?" Interest fired in her father's eyes.

"Yes, sir."

"I know his father. A good family man." He removed his frayed cap and ran a hand through his hair. "What if you were to marry Scott? Sounds like he has fine prospects now."

"Pa! I don't like him that way." Between her father's words and the way his hair stuck up at odd angles, he was like an alien to her.

"Scott is mighty keen on you," he continued. "I'm sure he would welcome your help with his studies."

Her mother rose and stepped to her side. Taking her hand, she said softly, "His father has raised the question, dear."

Ginger couldn't believe what she was hearing. She stepped back, recoiling at the idea. "I won't marry Scott. And I won't spend my life being a tutor to every man who is less intelligent than I am."

Her father scowled. "Why, you ungrateful child." Whipping his hand back, he advanced on her.

"Stu, don't," her mother shouted, grabbing his arm with surprising force. She cast a worried look at Ginger. "She's young. I'll talk to her."

Huffing and hitching up his stained trousers, her father seemed suddenly embarrassed at his outburst, but he covered it with his usual bluster. "Graduating from high school is an achievement for a woman. Look at your mother. You should be happy you don't have to leave school like she did."

Her father had never struck her, and she didn't think he would have, but Ginger knew she had touched a nerve. Yet, she had to make him understand how much she wanted— no, *deserved*, this chance. She had earned the privilege through diligence and determination.

Despite hot, angry tears threatening her eyes, Ginger drew herself up again. "Why do Calvin and Buford get to go? I'm smarter than they are. You've said so yourself."

Her father rubbed his forehead. "They need an education to improve their prospects and provide for the families they will have someday. Higher education is wasted on you."

"What if it were me that drowned instead of Jesse? You would send him." Even as the words left her mouth, she knew she had pushed too far.

Her mother was quick to step between them. "Stu, please don't. She didn't mean that."

With his face beet-red, her father jabbed a finger toward her. "My decision is final."

His words struck her harder than any blow he might have dealt. Ginger sucked in a breath and turned into her mother's protective embrace.

"There, there, dear," her mother murmured, encircling Ginger in her arms. "When you're married and raising your babies, you won't have time to think about anything else. And that time is not so far away."

"Mama, no," Ginger pleaded. "I can't get married, not yet."

Her father clenched his jaw while her mother tried again. "You don't want to miss finding a good man." She cast another look at her husband. "Maybe not Scott, but someone like him who would care for you."

Instead of encouragement, her mother's words sounded more like an apology. "I'm capable, and I can take care of myself."

Just then, Calvin came into the room, throwing a look at their father. "Hey, Ginger. Sure could use your help on my homework."

"She'll be right there," her mother said, her voice gaining strength. "Stu, go wash off that fishy smell while I start dinner."

Her father gave Ginger a final look of warning, and Calvin loped back to the room he shared with Buford.

When they were alone, her mother hugged Ginger to her chest and whispered into her thick mane of nutmeg-colored hair. "Scott was granted the scholarship I tried to get for you."

Ginger could hardly believe what she'd heard. "Why didn't you tell me you'd put me up for that?"

"I wanted to spare you the disappointment in case you weren't chosen," she whispered. "Don't tell your father. He would be furious."

Hope surged in Ginger's chest. "I could try for it next year."

Her mother shook her head. "The scholarship committee won't assist girls. But I'll help you get out of here."

"How?"

"I'm working on it with Miss Carter," her mother replied, her eyes blazing with determination. "You will not live the life I have."

Ginger opened her mouth to speak, but her mother pressed a finger to her lips. "That's enough for now. Go help your brother."

## 3

*T*he lunch run was long over, and Marina wondered where Jack was. He'd promised to meet her so they could look at new furnishings for their home. Then, she spied his car parked exactly where he'd left it earlier, near Ginger's cottage.

Had he spent all day with Ginger without a break?

Curious, she followed the path that connected the structures and opened the rear door to her grandmother's cottage. A deep conversation floated to her ears, and she made her way toward it.

"So you were disappointed that your father wouldn't let you continue your studies," Jack said.

"The Great Depression and the war took its toll on my family," Ginger replied, sounding practical. "Pa insisted my older brothers prepare for professions. There were no funds for my education."

Listening intently, Marina cut through the kitchen, past the red vintage O'Keefe & Merritt stove, and into the dining room. She recalled hearing Ginger tell that story with more emotion.

"Did you feel slighted?" Jack asked. "I know I would have."

Marina paused in the doorway to the study.

Catching a glimpse of Marina, Ginger nodded after a long moment. "At the time, I felt caged, furious, disappointed, and hurt. You see, I yearned for an education, not only for myself, but for what my younger brother Jesse would have had if he'd lived. He had a keen mind like mine."

Marina watched while Jack made notes. While still holding her posture erect, her grandmother seemed weary, as if she'd been speaking all day. Marina frowned with concern.

"Young women were presumed to marry instead, which I did. Father was hopelessly old-fashioned, even for that time." Ginger tapped her manicured nails on the table. "So, I simply got on with living."

Marina caught Ginger's eye and cleared her throat. "I remember how you read your brothers' books and skipped ahead in school."

"I'm delighted you were listening, Marina." A corner of her grandmother's mouth curved as she turned to Jack again. "From an early age, I set out to surpass my brothers and prove my intelligence to my father."

"That can be a strong motivation," Jack said, nodding.

"I'm sure I frightened him instead." A smile flitted across Ginger's face. "I devoured my brothers' academic books, determined to score high on challenge exams my teachers agreed to administer to me."

"What else drove you?" Jack asked. "Surely it was more than your father's approval."

Ginger appeared to reflect on that question for a moment. "I told myself I owed it to Jesse," she said slowly. "But I also had a pure thirst for knowledge."

Marina peered at the open photo album between them. She gestured beside a photo of two figures hunched over a game board. One of them was a very young Ginger. "What's the story behind this photo?"

"That was the day I won my first chess game against my father. My mother wanted to commemorate the occasion."

Marina smiled. "Your dad looks surprised and humbled."

"He certainly was." Ginger chuckled.

"You enjoyed intellectual games," Jack stated, leaning forward.

"More than that," Ginger replied. "Chess, calculus, codes, and ciphers. As a child, I hungered for the rewards of mental challenges. In my mind, that kept Jesse alive. Perhaps it was my way of making amends."

Knowing that was a tender subject, Marina touched her grandmother's shoulder. "Jack, you should know that Ginger's faculty with numbers spilled into other pursuits, too. She's a true renaissance woman."

Jack rolled his pen through his fingers. "In what ways—other than the obvious?"

"Take music, for example," Ginger said. "To me, music is auditory mathematics; baking, a precise experiment in chemical reactions; and fashion, architecture for the body. To discerning eyes, a sleeve or a hemline a finger's breadth too short or long will destroy the harmonious balance and line." She smiled fondly at a memory. "My mother shared these interests, too. She was a seamstress, but today, she might have been a top fashion designer."

Jack nodded and made another note. Glancing over his writings, he said, "You haven't told me how Jesse died."

"No, I haven't," Ginger replied, averting her gaze. "That is for another day."

Ginger suddenly seemed to shrink into herself, which alarmed Marina. She put a hand over Jack's notebook. "That's enough. Let her rest before dinner."

"Oh, sure," he said, glancing at his watch. "The time slipped away from us." Turning to Ginger, he asked, "Same time tomorrow?"

Her grandmother sighed, and Marina cut in, "You shouldn't meet every day. Why work so hard?"

Jack agreed, and Ginger pressed her fingers against Marina's arm in silent appreciation.

The last thing Marina wanted was for this project to burden Ginger. Jack didn't have a deadline for this manuscript. To her knowledge, he hadn't even pitched it to his agent.

Stealing another look at Ginger, she decided he must be more attuned to Ginger's emotional stamina, or she would halt these long sessions. As strong as her grandmother was, Marina would not allow Jack to wear her down. She would talk to him.

"I'll meet you at the house soon," Marina said.

He closed his notebook. "Sounds good. I'll pick up Leo on the way home."

After Jack left, Ginger motioned to a chair. "Stay for a moment."

Marina sank onto the chair beside her. "You two worked all day. Was that too much for you?"

"It wasn't too bad, but I was glad to see you," Ginger said, smoothing a hand over Marina's arm.

"I'll talk to Jack and ask him to slow down."

"I'm quite strong, dear. Don't think of me as feeble. However, some of my memories are emotionally draining."

"You hide it so well that no one notices." Marina patted Ginger's hand, which still looked strong and capable. "I'll make a pot of tea and bring dinner from the cafe for you and Heather. Vegetarian lasagna was the lunch special today."

"It's very much appreciated, my dear." She held her arms to Marina and hugged her.

A few minutes later, Marina left for home after delivering tea and supper. She was preparing a salad with the *gougères* and Cornish game hens she'd prepped this morning.

When Jack walked in alone, Marina looked up. "I thought you were picking up Leo?"

"I was, but Samantha's parents invited him for a beach barbecue. I couldn't top that, so I told him I'd see him tomorrow instead." A lazy smile touched his face. "Since we're alone, how about a glass of wine before dinner?"

"I'd love that. The Gruyère and Parmesan cheese bites you like are almost ready, too." She had put a trio of small, herb-encrusted hens into the oven. The extra one would be a good afternoon snack for Leo tomorrow. At eleven years old, he was ravenous, eating plenty to support his growth spurt. She would also steam broccoli and serve it over wild rice and toasted quinoa tonight.

Marina joined Jack on the front steps. She offered him

the plate of warm cheese bites, another specialty from Ginger. The land sloped toward the ocean so they could see the beach from here. In the distance, she saw Leo throwing a frisbee with Samantha, his best friend.

"Mmm, delicious." Jack handed her a glass of red wine. "How was your day?"

As she sipped the wine, she gave him a brief recap and then asked about his progress on Ginger's biography.

"We've only touched the surface of her life. That's the challenge of writing a story based on someone who has lived such a rich, varied life. Her story sounds like a sprawling saga, more like fiction than fact. I've been mesmerized all day."

Marina put her hand on Jack's knee. "About that...I want you to go easy on Ginger. Don't try to extract her entire life history in a few sittings. That's not the way she tells her story, but more than that, I'm afraid you might exhaust her."

Jack grinned. "She nearly wore me out today."

Marina shook her head. "You don't know her like I do. She was weary but was holding herself together for you. Ginger has tremendous stamina, but she likes a small nap in the afternoon to recharge. You didn't give her that chance today."

Immediately, Jack looked remorseful. "Honestly, I would have stopped if I thought she was waning. Now I feel terrible."

Leaning into him, Marina rubbed his shoulder. "It's okay, but please be careful with her. She has as much energy as people half her age but needs breaks. Everyone does, including you. I saw you stifling a yawn."

"I guess so," he admitted. "It's just that her story is so fascinating, and we're only at the beginning. When you look at her life in the context of history, you realize that she was at the forefront of many inventions, political developments, and social upheaval. Her story will be tremendously inspiring. And we haven't even gotten to her secret work yet."

Marina frowned at that. "She's family first. If she shares something that might put her at risk, remember that you don't have to include everything in the book."

Jack hugged her. "I promise."

"Are you sure?" She knew how dedicated Jack was to his profession.

He raised his hand. "I solemnly swear. Family comes first."

She accepted that, but still, she wondered if he could adhere to that promise. Jack was a professional known for being relentless and serving up the unvarnished truth. His investigative reporting had landed people in prison.

Marina had no idea what sort of secrets Ginger might have.

"Tomorrow, she promised to tell me how she met Bertrand."

"Not tomorrow." Marina nudged him.

"Oh, sorry," he said, looking apologetic. "Day after tomorrow, then."

Satisfied, Marina nodded. "That's a good story." However, she wondered if it would be the same as she knew. "And tread carefully about sensitive topics."

He kissed her cheek. "You can sit with us if you'd like."

"Maybe I will." Ginger was their treasure, and as much as she loved Jack, she wanted to ensure her grandmother was okay with his interview methods—not that Ginger couldn't handle Jack.

Two DAYS LATER, Marina joined Ginger and Jack in the comfortable living room at the cottage. They sat on the white canvas slip-covered sofa and chairs strewn with colorful beach pillows.

Marina leaned forward, touching Ginger's knee as she sat in a wingback chair, commanding the room like an empress. "Jack promised that he'll allow breaks whenever you want. And you're not to work long hours."

Jack nodded at her words. "My apologies for the other day, Ginger. I was engrossed in your story." He brought out a sepia photograph from the old album. "When we left off, you were about to talk about Jesse. Do you feel like starting there?"

Nodding, Ginger took the photo from him. "Jesse was such a dear." She studied the photo for a moment.

Marina looked at Jack. His attitude was much better than the other day.

Gesturing at the photograph, Ginger drew a breath. "This was the last happy day we were to know for some time. You see, Jesse drowned the next day."

"I'm so sorry," Jack said softly.

"Ginger, you don't have to talk about that," Marina interjected.

Her grandmother held up her hand. "It's alright. This is important for me to memorialize for the family."

"Only if you're sure," Marina added, glancing at Jack.

"You see, for a family who lived by the sea," Ginger

began, "I wondered how a soul I loved so dearly could succumb to a watery grave. We all knew better than to risk strong tides, but it happened in the blink of an eye. I was entirely unprepared for my brother's accident."

"How did it happen?" Jack asked gently.

Ginger smiled. "I once told my granddaughters that Jesse was swept away on angel's wings, but they were only children. Jesse and I had been playing catch on the beach. I was a little older, and I threw the ball harder than I should have to him. An offshore gust swept it even farther over the waves. Being close in age, we were quite competitive. He crashed into the water to retrieve it, ventured a little too far, and a riptide dragged him under."

Jack made a note and waited for her to continue.

"At that time, my thin, childish arms were no match for nature's raw power," Ginger continued. "I splashed after him but couldn't reach him. My youthful force of will wasn't enough to save him, and I was pulled under the surface as well. Somehow, I managed to scream for help above the roar of the waves."

Marina touched her shoulder. "You don't have to go on if you don't want to."

"Let me finish." Ginger drew a breath. "My father plucked me from the surf and threw me into my mother's arms before diving after Jesse. Mama always maintained that the extra second or two didn't matter; reaching my brother in time to save him had been impossible. So they saved me, even though I wished to trade places with Jesse."

"It wasn't your fault," Marina said. Now she knew why Ginger had insisted on early swim lessons when they were young and watched them closely at the beach.

"I always felt it was. I shouldn't have thrown the ball that hard near the waves. We weren't supposed to be that close to the ocean. Our parents looked away from us for only a few moments while unpacking the picnic. All these years, I've had tremendous guilt over this, yet I know my parents must have suffered even more."

Jack put down his notebook. "It was an unfortunate accident."

"I understand that now," Ginger said, her shoulders sloping as if from the burden she'd carried. "I certainly wasn't old enough to throw a ball with precision, and waves often catch adults off guard. After that, I swore to make it up to our parents by excelling in every endeavor and being the best daughter I could be. I vowed to live two lifetimes for us, more than a hundred years if I could."

"An extra lifetime for Jesse," Marina murmured. So this is what had been behind Ginger's childhood drive. *A vow to her brother.*

"I have certainly tried," Ginger said, touching a finger to the corner of her eye. "My goodness, I didn't realize recounting this story would affect me so."

"Let's take a break." Jack quickly handed Ginger a tissue while Marina stroked her hand.

Marina nodded, relieved that Jack wasn't pushing her grandmother anymore.

Ginger rose and excused herself. "When I return, I'll tell you all about Bertrand. That's a much happier story, I promise."

## 4

"Whatever they ask if you can do, say yes." Mary Lou touched Ginger's shoulder as she spoke. "Typing, filing, dictation, and shorthand—"

"What is shorthand?" Ginger asked, looking between her mother and Beatrice Carter, her trusted teacher. They sat in Miss Carter's classroom after school hours.

"A type of rapid writing," Beatrice replied, lowering her glasses. "You will learn it quickly. Until then, take notes as you would in class." She held up a finger and smiled. "Whatever they dictate, it won't hurt to make it sound better than what they might have said."

"Thank you, Miss Carter." Ginger admired her teacher, who always seemed to have the answers. Beatrice Carter was the most capable, accomplished woman she knew. "What else might I be asked to do?"

Beatrice sighed. "You'll probably be asked to make coffee or have lunch brought in. But never do anything against your better judgment, no matter how attractive the man might be. Morally speaking, I mean."

"Of course not," Ginger replied, surprised at that. She fiddled with the top button on the starched white shirt her mother had made.

She glanced at her mother, who nodded solemnly and returned her attention to the teacher.

"With your height, you look older, and with your bright ginger hair, you'll stand out among the applicants," Beatrice said. "Make sure your intelligence shines through. That will set you apart from other young ladies. Most of them will not have a background in science or mathematics, and certainly not to your level."

"How many appointments have you scheduled for me?" Ginger asked.

"Two, so far," Beatrice replied, glancing at her notepad. "Both are in Los Angeles. I know a woman at the California Museum of Science and Industry. She is expecting you. I have also arranged an interview with a man who consults for IBM, although that might require travel to New York at some point."

"Absolutely not," her mother said with a stern expression.

"Mrs. Sheraton, it would be an excellent opportunity for her."

Mary Lou frowned, looking conflicted. "What is this IBM?"

"It stands for International Business Machines," Beatrice replied.

Ginger looked doubtful. "Business? I don't know anything about that."

"They need mathematicians for the computers they are developing," Beatrice replied.

That sounded exciting to Ginger. "They'll pay me to do that?"

Beatrice shook her head. "This is for a secretarial position. First, you must prove yourself efficient, indispensable, and of good character. Then, you'll find a chance to show them what you can do. In the meantime, keep studying. And keep your eyes open for opportunity."

"A chance is all I want." Excitement sizzled in Ginger's chest. "I wish I could tell Pa about this."

"Once you have a job, I'll tell him," her mother said, sounding weary.

"Yes, ma'am." Ginger folded her hands in her lap. Her mother had pleaded with her to be on her best behavior with her father until she had secured a position.

Beatrice brought out a folder. "I took the liberty of securing applications for you. Your mother can help you complete these. Where it asks your age, put down eighteen."

Ginger's heart plummeted. "But that would be lying. I'm sixteen-and-a-half."

"You're tall enough to be considered eighteen." Beatrice glanced at Mary Lou.

"It was a home birth," her mother said quickly. "There might have been a mistake on the year. I can correct that."

"But Mama," Ginger whispered, mortified at what her mother suggested.

Mary Lou glanced at Beatrice. "Would you excuse us one moment, Miss Carter?"

"You stay here. I need a break anyway." Her teacher rose and excused herself, closing the door behind her.

Ginger shifted uncomfortably in her seat. "I'm not going to lie."

Her mother sighed heavily. "Your father is arranging your marriage."

"I'm not getting married either," Ginger said, folding her arms.

"Your choices are limited," her mother replied, pitching forward in the hard wooden chair. "That's why we're here. Miss Carter believes in your ability. You are so much like my father; you have his brain. But your father will never understand how much more you could be." An unwavering expression sharpened her words. "You must seize what opportunities you can. I'm an honest woman, but if you choose to marry that dreadful young man your father picked for you, I will—"

"I'm eighteen, Mama," Ginger said, nearly trembling at her mother's fierce determination. "I remember now." Like her mother, she would do whatever it took to secure this chance.

Beatrice returned with a slip of paper for them. "Here are the addresses. Your mother will go with you on the train and wait while you have your interviews. I have written letters of reference, which both parties have already received. And I wish you the very best of luck. It has been a pleasure being your teacher."

Ginger embraced her. "Thank you, Miss Carter. I understand everything."

. . .

OUTSIDE THE FANCY office on Wilshire Boulevard, Ginger paused to steady her nerves. She clutched the black leather purse her mother had given her.

"Hold your head high and enter first," Mary Lou said. "You can manage this. They'll be lucky to have you."

Ginger strode into the office, hardly believing she was there. Other young women sat waiting in a line of chairs, their perfume heady in the enclosed area. One man in a suit smoked while he read a newspaper. Typewriters clacked in a nearby room, and a telephone rang at the front desk. She paused, waiting for the receptionist, who answered the phone in a chirpy voice. She looked only a few years older than Ginger.

After giving her name, Ginger said, "I'm here to interview with Mr. Kurt Powell."

Her mother had followed her into the waiting room. She wore her Sunday best dress with her only pair of pumps. Ginger wore a taupe skirt, an ivory blouse she'd made herself, and a rose-colored sweater her mother had knitted.

"I will let him know you're here." The woman peered around her. "May I help you, ma'am?"

"Thank you, but I'm with my daughter," Mary Lou said. "I'll wait here for her."

Ginger clutched her application, taking care not to crease it. She sat beside her mother. If she got this position, she would live with a cousin on her mother's side. How quickly her life would change.

She took her mother's hand. In a whisper, she said, "Thank you for this. Pa will be very angry, won't he?"

Mary Lou leaned toward her. "We both want what's best for you."

"But you have different ideas about that."

"You should have all the opportunities you can manage. That's what I want for you. When you're ready to marry, it will be to a man you love. That's too important of a decision to leave to someone else." She paused, pressing Ginger's hand for emphasis. "You have a fine mind, but you must also learn to trust your instincts. You're in the city now."

Another woman appeared, and the receptionist signaled to her. "Miss Mary Ellen, please follow Mrs. Bingham. Mr. Powell will see you now."

Carefully balancing on her new pumps, Ginger followed the other woman.

As they walked through the hall, laughter spilled from an office. The other woman paused at the door, announced Ginger, and introduced Mr. Powell, a clean-cut man in a fine dark suit. Not unattractive, Ginger noted, but she wasn't there to make such observations.

"I am pleased to meet you and thank you for seeing me." She handed him her application. While Mr. Powell perused her information, she glanced toward another man who waited in an adjoining seating area. The beautifully decorated office featured a polished wooden desk with a hunter-green leather top, thick wool rugs, leather chairs, and a brocade sofa.

She had never seen anything like this.

Mr. Powell nodded and looked up, seemingly satisfied with her courses of study. "Have a seat, Miss Sheraton. Do you mind if I call you Grace?"

"I do, Mr. Powell." She lifted her chin, determined to make a good impression. Still, it was imperative she be treated with respect, as her mother insisted. "I prefer Ginger."

The man looked impressed with her forthrightness. "And I'm partial to Kurt. Now that we have that settled let's talk about the position. Beatrice Carter speaks highly of your skills. She considers you at the pinnacle of the students she has taught."

*Past tense*, Ginger noted, so she played along. "I enjoyed her class."

Kurt splayed his hands on his desk. "We met when I gave a presentation at her alma mater. Since then, she has sent her brightest minds to me. I need smart young women with talents other than typing and filing."

Was this one of the trick questions Miss Carter had warned her about? "I excel in mathematics. And science."

"And English?"

"Top marks." She wasn't bragging—that would be unseemly. She was only stating a fact. Mrs. Windsor had rigorously enforced the study of English grammar, composition, diction, and rhetoric in her class and insisted students elevate the art of speech and pronunciation.

Kurt laced his fingers. "And what do you do in your spare time?"

"I read, and I like to solve puzzles." She relaxed a little; she had practiced this response.

A smile touched his lips as if he found that amusing. "Like crossword or jigsaw puzzles?"

"Oh, they're alright. I meant codes and ciphers. My

young brother and I once created a secret written language."

The other man looked up with interest, and Kurt said, "Your brother sounds as smart as you are."

"Yes, he was." Ginger was caught off guard this time, so she didn't elaborate.

Kurt acknowledged that detail with a nod. "Good problem solvers are hard to find. Not many people look beyond the obvious."

"No, sir. But they should."

Kurt chuckled. "You're direct. I like that. Now, I'll tell you about the project I need help on. Do you know the meaning of data encryption?"

"It's a process of encoding information in cryptography." Relishing the conversation, Ginger leaned forward so she wouldn't miss anything.

He lifted his brow and nodded. "I'm a consultant to the head of IBM and branches of the military. I work on projects for the company involving the development and use of new technologies. I imagine this is why Miss Carter recommended you so strongly. I often travel to New York and Chicago, so you'll need winter clothes if I hire you. Can you manage that?"

Ready for any change, she looked at him squarely in the eye. "The travel or the wardrobe?"

Looking slightly amused, Kurt steepled his hands and peered at her. "Both."

"I can manage both, sir."

He grinned. "You pay attention to the details. That's good. You'll meet a lot of interesting characters. Starting with my friend from Harvard, Bertrand Delavie."

"How do you do?" she said automatically as the other man acknowledged her, touching his forehead in a gracious gesture.

Kurt motioned toward an open door past Bertrand. "You'll work in that adjoining office."

Ginger wasn't sure what he meant. "Do you wish to hire me?"

"If you want the job, I just did," Kurt replied with a small smile. "You may start on Monday."

"I can start today."

"Monday will be soon enough." Kurt jerked a thumb toward his friend. "I have to show this wandering cowboy around town."

"You're a cowboy?" she asked the other man, intrigued. The description didn't fit with his manner or attire.

Bertrand grinned and wagged his head at his friend. "Kurt means that I'm always eager to travel, among other things. I work in diplomacy."

"Which means Bertrand spends most of his time outside the country," Kurt said.

"Only to stay clear of you, old man."

Bertrand spoke with an accent that wasn't from this coast. She had never met anyone like him. How he spoke and lived was fascinating. And he was a good ten years older than she was. She returned her attention to her new boss. "If that's all, I should be on my way so you can continue your work."

"Then it's settled." When Kurt rose, so did Bertrand. He shook her hand and promised he'd see her Monday morning.

Ginger was thrilled and delighted, as was her mother.

After much persuading by Mary Lou, Ginger's father accepted her work grudgingly, although he disapproved of it.

Nevertheless, Ginger immersed herself in a new world and loved it. Kurt treated her as an equal, though she had much to learn. In her free time, she devoured books on various subjects, including mathematics, engineering, and emerging computational technologies.

When Kurt's friend Bertrand visited, he often invited her for coffee in the diner in the building, insisting Kurt didn't pay her enough, which Ginger protested against. Still, buying coffee for her soon became a regular occurrence when Bertrand was in town.

When Kurt traveled on business to New York, he brought Ginger, and she often met Bertrand for coffee in the hotel. He told her he was committed to helping her navigate her new surroundings and protect her from unsavory sorts.

Mary Lou was delighted to learn a man of Bertrand's stature was looking out for her daughter. Ginger told her that he was always correct with her, which was true. She enjoyed their intelligent conversations. There was no one she'd rather spend time with, so she turned down invitations from other young men who seemed to have different ideas in mind. Her time was too precious to waste.

GINGER AND BERTRAND had known each other for two years when he asked if she would accompany him to an event hosted by the American ambassador to France. Kurt had business in New York with IBM. As usual, she was there to assist him and take notes.

"Before you answer, I would like you to attend as my date," Bertrand said, stirring his coffee. "People will assume that, so I wanted to clarify. You may take a few days to think about it. If you don't wish to go, I'll accept that."

However, the idea appealed to Ginger. She sat up straighter at the table. "I understand. I don't need time."

Bertrand drew his brow. "Then, you'll go as my date?"

"Yes. I would like to see what one does on a date." She'd seen couples on the silver screen and heard the gossip of other secretaries, so she was somewhat prepared.

"I hope you're not disappointed." Bertrand chuckled. "You're a rare treasure, dear Ginger. I knew it the first moment I saw you in Kurt's office. Now, you'll need a specific type of dress, so I will make an appointment for you at a store where I shop."

She arched an eyebrow. "Surely not for men's clothing?"

"They have a department for ladies. You'll be in good hands, I assure you."

When Ginger visited the store with multiple departments, the saleswoman treated her like visiting royalty. While models paraded the clothes she had selected for Ginger, the woman served tea in thin teacups and offered her cucumber sandwiches. The woman told Ginger that Mr. Delavie insisted on paying for her evening gown. It seemed a waste of energy to disagree, so Ginger selected a mint-green dress she thought Bertrand would like that also accented her hair.

She could hardly wait for their first date.

5

*W*hile Cruise managed the cafe kitchen on slow afternoons, Marina tended to business and developed new recipes. Today, she worked on fresh salmon sliders in Ginger's cottage. She loved working where she'd learned to cook alongside her grandmother during summer visits.

"Coleslaw, tomato, blackened salmon, homemade herb buns," she said to herself as she wrote down the ingredients and took a photo. Marina was trying different flavor profiles and standardizing new recipes for the food truck side of her business.

Kai swept into the kitchen. She was a vision in a leopard print catsuit, proudly showing her baby bump.

Looking up, Marina grinned. "Wowzer, that's some outfit, Mama."

Kai lowered her dark sunglasses onto her nose. "This kid will be born with theatrical style." She pulled out her phone. "Did you see your video on social media?"

"You know I don't look at that anymore." Starting another version of her recipe, Marina sprinkled minced rosemary from the garden into a small bowl of panko and shredded salmon.

Kai stared at her. "Since when?"

"Since my on-air blooper became a meme." Marina could laugh about it now, but that had marked a tragic end to her anchor position and broadcasting career. "I couldn't bear to see it plastered everywhere. The comments were awful. But that's all behind me now."

Kai slid her phone across the kitchen counter. "Not so fast. It's a powerful medium. Just look at all these comments. You *have* to write that cookbook now."

Marina started to turn away, but the video caught her eye, and she was shocked at what she saw. The clip began with Jack dipping her low while they danced. Kai had floated words across the top: *Hot moves in the kitchen at the Coral Cafe!*

Marina couldn't bear to look at the comments, though she was curious—and concerned. She had invested a lot in the cafe and didn't want strangers' comments to damage her business. "Kai, I didn't know you'd filmed that part. What are people saying?"

"Chill, Marina." Kai massaged her shoulders. "They're all good comments. I teased them, too, saying you were working on a cookbook. How quickly can you throw one together, do you think?"

"Even with Heather's help, it won't happen overnight." Marina shrugged away from Kai, appalled at her sister's actions. She formed the salmon patties, drizzled olive oil in a sauté pan, and adjusted the flame. "I'm super busy right now. The loan went through for another food truck. It will be outfitted, and I need to hire and train staff."

"People only want to know if they can reserve copies of your upcoming cookbook. I think you should take preorders."

"You put all that in the video?"

"People love the behind-the-scenes clips," Kai replied. "And the bloopers. But the best one is when Jack sweeps you off your feet. He's their new heartthrob."

Marina placed the patties into the sizzling oil. "Wait until Jack hears about this."

"Are you kidding? He loves it."

"You showed it to him already?"

"I was waiting for the cafe to slow down. He and Leo were there, so I sat with them. When I opened my phone, he asked what I was laughing about. I couldn't stop checking because it was blowing up with comments."

"I don't want to see any of them." Those on her video that went viral had lodged in her mind. Even though she'd developed a thick skin from working in the news, she was still human and had feelings. She had no idea how celebrities lived with people's insensitive comments about them.

Kai made a face. "I thought you'd be happy. You have no idea how big this is. You're going viral again."

Marina shuddered. "I hope it's better than last time."

"Oh, it is. You can take this one to the bank." Kai wiggled her fingers. "Cha-ching, cha-ching."

It wasn't a bad idea. Marina grinned at Kai's enthusiasm. "All I have to do is write an entire book."

"Get Ginger to help you test recipes," Kai said, doing a little shimmy. "She'd love to have a project."

Just then, Ginger entered the kitchen. She wore wide-legged cotton trousers, a matching taupe jacket, and pearls. Marina knew this was one of her grandmother's vintage outfits, but it was still a lovely classic.

"Did I just hear my name bandied about?" Ginger asked.

Marina flipped the salmon, then jotted a note in her food notebook. "My sister is making more work for me and threatening to pull you into it. Be careful; it's hot in here."

Kai spread her hands. "So, I posted a few video clips from the shoot. People are going wild over the idea that Marina is writing a cookbook and are eager to preorder. The publicity for the cafe would be huge."

"It sounds like a marvelous idea," Ginger said.

Marina lifted the pan from the burner. "Except that I have very little time to start another project. That's when Kai served you up for the task."

"I would be delighted," Ginger said. "Challenge accepted. I have so many recipes we could include."

Marina smiled at her enthusiasm. "Heather volunteered to organize my recipes and draft new material. All the recipes should be dishes we serve at the cafe. I've changed many of your original ones. I use less butter and oil and more fresh ingredients. People want healthier food options today than those of the 1960s."

"Many, yes, but you're generalizing," Ginger said. "You've already done the hard work. You could even dictate the text."

Ginger's eyes blazed with such happiness that Marina couldn't deny her this project. She'd meant to write a cookbook someday with recipes from the cafe, but something had always come up.

"Are you sure you'd have time?" Marina squinted at Ginger. "You're already working with Jack on your biography."

Ginger waved a hand. "My dear, I do very little. I tell him stories and show him a few photographs. Jack is piecing it all together and writing. Creating a cookbook with you and Heather would be a welcome treat."

Marina plated the sliders and passed them around. This may be the right time. Her grandmother was in excellent health. Ginger could live to be a hundred or more given her healthy lifestyle.

Still, Marina couldn't take her for granted, and the years had a way of barreling along like a freight train. It seemed only yesterday that her twins were toddlers.

"I'll print some recipes from the current menu that Cruise uses," Marina said. "We'll have to adjust the amounts for home cooking."

Ginger's eyes glittered. "Fortunately, you have a writing partner who is also a mathematician. I will make the adjustments and test the recipes."

Heather sauntered in the kitchen. "Are we recipe testing again? That's my favorite."

Kai wiggled in a little happy dance. "Ginger agreed to help you and Marina write the cookbook. Want to help me set up a website page to take preorders?"

"Sure," Heather replied. Marina offered her a salmon slider, and she scooped it up. "Count me in, but I have to go. Blake is picking me up any minute."

"And how is your young man?" Ginger asked.

Heather smiled, and her face flushed pink with happiness. "We're really happy."

Kai nudged her. "What exactly does that mean?"

Ignoring her aunt, Heather bit into the slider. "Mmm, this is delicious, Mom. I like the coleslaw and the blackened fish. Our customers would love this."

Ginger lifted her chin toward the window. "Here's Blake now."

"Could I have another one for him, Mom? We're going to a beach barbecue, but it could be hours before the food is ready."

"Sure," Marina replied. "I'd like his opinion, too." She would consider each dish on taste, presentation, ease of preparation, and cost.

Marina watched as Heather waved Blake inside through the kitchen door. He was a good-looking aquatic veterinarian with closely cropped hair and a fine physique. Since he'd moved to Summer Beach a few months ago to head ocean rescue operations, the two of them had spent a lot of time together. Still, Blake insisted that Heather keep up with her homework. Marina liked that about him.

When Blake stepped inside, Heather stood on her tiptoes and kissed his cheek. "I have something for you. We're recipe testing. Are you hungry?"

He grinned. "I'm famished. My team had to rescue a sea lion today, so we worked through lunch."

Marina served up more sliders, and soon everyone was tasting them and offering opinions. "I'll make some adjustments on the next batch." She made a few more notes.

Ginger turned to Kai. "I'd like to see this video you mentioned."

"Not in the kitchen," Marina said, waving them away.

"She's still a little sensitive," Kai said in a loud stage whisper. "Come with me."

Ginger and Heather followed Kai into the dining room, though Blake stayed behind. He rocked on his heels and cleared his throat, looking a little nervous.

"Is there something on your mind?" Marina asked.

"I know you're busy, but I'd like to speak to you some time."

"Is this about Heather?"

He nodded, seeming oddly unsure of himself.

That was not like the Blake she knew. Marina's senses went on high alert. "Is she okay?"

"She's not in any trouble, if that's what you're asking. She's doing well in school, and she's, uh, healthy. Very healthy," he stammered.

"I'm glad to hear that." Marina wondered what was going on. "How about later this week? I can leave the kitchen in the later afternoon."

"Perfect," he replied, looking relieved.

Kai and the others returned to the kitchen, smiling but trying not to show it too much.

Heather hooked her arm through Blake's. "We'll see you all later." She waved, and they went out the door.

Ginger peered at Marina. "Why are you looking so odd?"

Marina chewed the side of her lip. "Blake wants to talk to me. He probably wants to ask if we're doing anything for Heather's birthday. And Ethan's, of course. Maybe he wants to throw a surprise party or have it at the cafe."

Kai placed a hand over her heart and swooned. "Or whisk her off to somewhere wildly romantic."

"And look where that got you," Marina said, nodding toward Kai's abdomen.

"Heather is next," Kai said, laughing.

Marina shook a spatula at her sister. "Don't even say that. Heather has plenty of time before settling down with someone."

"Even if it's Mr. Dreamy Sea Vet?" Kai asked.

"She's still in school," Marina replied firmly. "May we please get off this conversation?"

Ginger put her arm around Kai. "Dear, would you teach me how to use that dictation you mentioned? I'd like to write a letter to an old friend."

Kai smiled. "Would that be Oliver?"

"Well, as it happens, yes." Ginger's expression bloomed at his name. "He called to see if I planned to attend the celebration of life. I told him I would. I'd like to write a few remembrances of his brother and send that to him."

"That's thoughtful," Marina said. Ginger's voice held a certain lightness she hadn't heard in a long time, and she wondered how close she had been to Oliver.

Kai put an arm around Ginger. "Let's go figure this out."

After they left the room, Marina gazed out the window toward the beach, her thoughts returning to Heather and Blake. Kai was wrong about them. Her daughter would have confided in her if they were that close. She was sure of that.

And yet, Blake had been uncharacteristically nervous.

## 6

*T*he salty ocean breeze tousled Ginger's hair as she strolled along the sun-drenched beach beside Jack, enjoying the cool morning air. "Next time, we'll hike to the ridgetop. Life is long; stay as active as you can."

Jack adjusted the brim of his cap. "We all try to keep up with you."

"Don't patronize me." Ginger slid him a look of mild reproach. "I know you're taking it easy on me. You must learn that productivity is about efficiency and effectiveness, not maximizing the hours you invest in a task. Life should be enjoyed as well. The Europeans know that far better than us—I learned that in Paris. Make sure to include that in the manuscript."

"Will do," Jack said. "That's good advice."

She breathed deeply, savoring the scent of freshly baked muffins drifting from the cafe. Marina and Heather were preparing for an early brunch special. Though she'd lived in this seaside village for decades, the sights and smells of the beach always lifted her spirits.

She had always loved coming home to Summer Beach.

Jack whistled to Scout, who was circling a mound of seaweed that had washed onto the shore. "Leave it, boy."

Scout's ears pricked up. At the sound of Jack's voice, he circled back.

Ginger laughed as he loped toward them with his endearing awkward gait, his paws leaving a winding trail in the wet sand. "That dog is a real treasure. A true companion."

"Leo sure loves him." Jack flicked a stick for Scout to fetch. "My old life was nothing compared to what I have now with him and Marina. And the entire family. I appreciate you welcoming me into the fold."

"I had faith in you, even if you were a rough diamond at the time."

Just ahead, the mayor jogged along the hard-packed sand. "Good morning, you two," Bennett called with a wide grin.

Ginger nodded while Jack greeted him. Her new son-in-law had made friends and settled nicely into Summer Beach. She was pleased, especially for Marina and the twins.

"Where would you like to begin today?" she asked.

"The last time we spoke, you said you wanted to share more about you and Bertrand."

Ginger blinked against a rush of memories. She paused, carefully considering what she planned to share with Jack. How much of her story did she need to include? She gazed out to sea, considering where to start.

Surfers bobbed in the water in wetsuits, waiting for the sets of waves worth their effort. They'd probably been in the water since first light, chasing the prime morning waves. She recalled her free-spirited youth growing up here. And her return trips, each one punctuating a different chapter in her life.

Jack tried again. "You mentioned Paris. Tell me about your time there."

"I will, but we're not there yet." Her memories would be lost if she didn't share her story with him. She wanted to leave her family with the knowledge of her life. Perhaps that was a little vain, although her grandfather's life had inspired her. Maybe her great-grandchildren would be inspired by hers.

With a fortifying breath, she began.

"While working in Los Angeles for Kurt Powell, my horizons expanded, and I longed for more adventures. Every day was a chance for reinvention, far from my parents' watchful eyes and expectations."

"Let's back up," Jack said. "When did your parents arrive here? I'm also trying to put this in the context of Summer Beach history."

"My parents arrived in the 1920s," she replied. "The fresh ocean breezes and pristine beach attracted them, especially after their dry, dust-laden farm in Oklahoma. They started fresh here. My father knew someone who had moved earlier and had built up a small fleet of fishing vessels. Around that time, other people from Los Angeles and San Francisco built summer cottages here. That included the Ericksons, who constructed their grand summer home, Las Brisas del Mar."

"When did you buy the Coral Cottage?"

"You're getting ahead of yourself again." She angled toward a flat rock on the beach overlooking the ocean. "Let's sit there."

They eased onto the rock, and Jack brought out his phone. "Mind if I record this?"

"It's better that you do. I don't want you to miss anything important."

Jack tapped the record button on his phone. "Let's pick up from wherever you feel comfortable."

Ginger brought up her denim-clad legs and clasped her arms around her knees. "As you know, I worked for Kurt Powell, Bertrand's closest friend from his university days. Oh my, what an exciting position I had. Kurt was at the technological forefront with clients such as IBM and the United States Armed Forces. The early days of computers were heady, indeed. I continued enhancing my mathematical skills and studied early computer languages—even helped develop some."

She shared a few more details, glad that Jack was recording this. Memories were popping into her head so fast she could hardly keep up with the mental editing process.

When she paused, Jack asked, "If it's not too personal, may I ask how you and Bertrand began courting?"

Ginger touched his shoulder and laughed at his use of the old term. "Courting sounds so elegant and romantic. It's one of those words that should come back into vogue, like pearls and martinis. In my mind, dating doesn't have the same formality or intent about it, and certainly not as a prerequisite for a grand love affair, which is what we had."

"Courting...pearls and martinis...what a quote," Jack said, chuckling with her. "May I use that?"

"I hope you do." Ginger tipped her face to the cool morning breezes, relishing her memories. "Bertrand and I were friends for two years before he invited me to an ambassador's party in New York. That's when our relationship shifted. Why, I remember it like it was yesterday..."

———————

IN HER HOTEL room in New York, Ginger smoothed her hands over the soft emerald silk of her exquisite evening gown. The delicate embroidery woven with metallic thread caught the light as she moved, making the dress shimmer like a thousand jewels.

She could scarcely believe this was her reflection in the mirror. Her light auburn hair was swept up in an elegant updo, courtesy of a talented hairdresser in the hotel beauty parlor, which was so fancy it had a chandelier in the entryway.

Her boss enjoyed staying in the finest hotels, and Kurt Powell kept a busy schedule. Generally, she was on her own for dinner, which she liked to take in her room or at a cafe downstairs. She was uneasy about venturing out in the city by herself. Besides, she needed the time to continue her studies.

Not tonight, however.

Ginger turned in front of the mirror, taking in the full effect. Surprisingly, she looked like the sophisticated young woman she longed to become. She hoped Bertrand would be pleased with her transformation.

She thought of the dark skirts and pumps she usually wore to the office. She'd taken her fashion cues from other women who worked in the office, emulating the most successful senior secretaries and office manager.

Still, she couldn't resist adding a splash of color to her outfits with scarves around her neck. She bought remnants of silk at the fabric shop near where she lived with her cousin and learned how to roll and stitch the hems as they did in Italy.

Her guilty pleasures were the fashion magazines other secretaries left in the lunchroom. With the discerning eye of a seamstress developed under her mother's tutelage, she studied the latest styles, the drape of fabric, and pleasing silhouettes on the glossy pages.

Her style was changing, and she liked what she saw in the mirror now.

What intrigued her even more were people's reactions to style. The more senior a secretary, the less embellished their clothing. They wore clothing her mother would call tasteful and polished.

Not that she planned to be a secretary for any longer than necessary. She was eager for a chance to use her mathematical skills.

The hotel phone rang. "Miss Sheraton? You have a guest waiting for you in the lobby."

"I'll be right down. Thank you." Asking Bertrand to meet her upstairs at her room would have been inappropriate; the hotel frowned on that.

She picked up the small evening bag the saleswoman had suggested. Fortunately, the woman had organized her entire outfit, including shoes, hosiery, and special undergarments. Pausing by the mirror, she thought of her mother. Mary Lou Sheraton would have been proud of her. She could hardly wait to write to her and tell her all about this magical evening.

Stepping into the elevator, she nodded to the uniformed attendant, an older man who smiled at her appearance. "Lobby, please."

"Looks like this is a very special evening for you," he said, admiring her dress.

"It's my first date," she confided in him, hardly able to contain her excitement. She would have preferred to tell her mother, but long-distance telephone calls were expensive. Her mother would have chastised her for that, so Ginger would send her a letter with all the details about the evening instead. She enjoyed writing and bringing her travels to life for her mother.

"A special night to remember," the man said as he selected the floor.

While the elevator slid downstairs, Ginger's heart quickened with anticipation. This evening promised to be one beyond her dreams.

The elevator doors opened to the ornate gilded lobby, where fashionable people chatted among fine upholstered furnishings. In one corner, a pianist played classical music.

Nearby, the man responsible for her fairytale transformation awaited her. Bertrand Delavie, looking devastatingly handsome in a bespoke tuxedo, approached her and took her hand. His silver-gray eyes sparkled with surprise, admiration...and something else.

*Unmistakable affection.*

"You're utterly breathtaking," he murmured with a

whisper of a kiss to her outstretched hand. "I will be the envy of every man this evening."

Her cheeks warmed at his words. Deflecting his comments, she said, "Your saleswoman has a magic wand. I don't know how to thank you for this indulgence."

Bertrand continued holding her hand. "It's my unparalleled pleasure."

Feeling the heat of his skin on hers, she tried to draw a breath but felt a constriction in her chest. Their usual friendly banter over coffee was already going differently this evening.

This was a date with a capital D. He'd been quite clear about that.

But why was her heart racing and her breathing so shallow? This sudden change in her physiology made little sense to her.

Pressing a hand to her collarbone, she said, "Everything feels different about tonight." She weighed the variables that had changed to ascertain which one was having this impact on her. "Is it what we're wearing?"

A smile played on Bertrand's lips. "It might be. We're looking our best this evening."

Nodding, she replied, "I wouldn't think clothes would make such a difference, but they seem to."

"The right clothes inspire confidence. You're more stunning than you realize."

The heartbeat in his hand intensified, although it wasn't in the least unpleasant. "Then what is it? Why the sudden shift between us?"

Bertrand ran a hand over his face in a not-so-subtle attempt to hide his humor, although Ginger failed to see what he found funny. "It's not what is on the outside but the inside. In our hearts, dear Ginger. I believe we are fonder of each other than you realized."

"Thank you for that insight," Ginger replied, appreciating the sense in that. "You might be right."

"Then, let our evening begin." He presented his arm, and she slid her hand into the crook of his elbow as she'd seen women do in the movies. He guided her to a chauffeured car that awaited them and, with a gesture to the driver, insisted on helping her inside.

Flushed with pleasure, Ginger beamed at him.

On the drive to the French ambassador's Connecticut home, their conversation relaxed into a more familiar rhythm, yet she still detected something akin to an energetic attraction between them.

When they arrived, Bertrand took Ginger's hand again. Together, they ascended the steps to a grand estate and crossed the threshold into a world of grandeur.

The soaring ceilings, glittering crystal chandeliers, and impeccably dressed attendees immediately transported Ginger's imagination to the lavish party scenes described in *The Great Gatsby*, the book she'd recently devoured. However, with her sensibilities, she was confident the ending to her evening would be quite different.

She clung tighter to Bertrand's arm, taking in the splendor surrounding them. With Bertrand by her side, she felt at ease. Servers with trays of champagne and interesting bite-sized portions of food circulated among the guests, and he took a pair of glasses for them.

"You may sip this," he whispered. "But it might make you a little light-headed. You don't have to finish it."

She sipped through the bubbles, delighted at the fizzy nature of the golden champagne. She could imagine her mother's reaction to this. "Thank you for the warning."

As they wove through the crowd, he introduced her as his date, alternating seamlessly between English and French, rendering even the simplest of greetings eloquent.

"How did you learn French?" Ginger asked, intrigued. She hadn't known he spoke the language.

"Originally from my grandparents. I also studied languages in school."

"Do you know others?"

"A smattering of a variety," he replied modestly. Turning slightly, he acknowledged a man nearby. "Now, I would like to introduce you to our hosts."

The ambassador beamed at Bertrand. "My dear friend. It's wonderful to see you." His eyes twinkled as he turned to Ginger. "And who is this enchanting young lady?"

"Ambassador DuBois, may I present Miss Ginger Sheraton." Bertrand placed a hand on the small of her back. "Ginger, this is Ambassador DuBois and his wife, Marie."

Marie greeted her warmly in lightly accented English. "What a pleasure to meet you, Miss Sheraton. We're delighted you could join us this evening."

They chatted, and then the two men began to speak about world affairs. While Marie excused herself to welcome other guests, Ginger followed the conversation with keen interest. Far from feeling left out, she was thrilled to be in the company of such intelligent men. How refreshing it was, and how different from the small beach town where she'd grown up.

Shortly, they moved into another resplendent room. A

multi-course meal followed, and Ginger analyzed every dish. Conversations were grounded in importance—far from the frivolous talk of the secretarial staff. She delighted in the exchange of thoughtful opinions and the desire for real solutions to improve world situations. They spoke of using new technologies and industrial innovation to address topics as diverse as space travel, democracy, and hunger.

This was the world she was meant for. She could feel it.

More than that, she knew she could contribute to it.

After dinner, couples took to the dance floor, swaying to a small orchestra. Bertrand leaned in. "Are you enjoying yourself, *ma chérie?*" he asked, lightly caressing her knuckles with his thumb.

"It's magical," she replied. All evening, his merest glance or touch sent shivers through her. At first, the physiological response surprised her, but as the hours passed, she became more accustomed to it. "The finery and food are astounding, but it's the conversation and ideas I find most stimulating."

"You're a rare one, Ginger." A slow smile curved Bertrand's lips as he leaned his head toward hers.

"We're all unique."

"Indeed we are, but you stand far above the rest. Would you care to dance?"

She must have looked doubtful because he whispered, "Simply follow my lead. A waltz is a box step. Listen to the music and move with me." His eyes twinkling, he stood and offered his hand.

Her long skirt swirled around her calves as she moved with the swelling music, his arms embracing her at a respectable distance. She fell into step with him, recalling

the simple four-step movement from a school dance she'd
once attended. Not that she'd danced then; she'd towered
over the other boys, and none dared ask her to dance. Still,
she'd watched and memorized the steps. Those young
couples were far from adept, paling compared to those who
glided with ease around her now.

Four simple steps—easy math. Insofar as music was
based on math, so were the dances accompanying it. She
relaxed into the rhythm.

Bertrand kept eye contact, seemingly amused at something that escaped her. Yet, an inexplicable warmth filled
her chest. As much as she enjoyed their previous casual
conversations, tonight was an altogether different
experience.

In his arms, her feelings for him grew. She had come to
know this man over countless coffees, and she felt safe in his
arms.

At once, she knew. This is where she was meant to be.
They danced until, finally, he whispered, "We should go.
One shouldn't be among the last to leave a party. I like to
leave people wishing I'd stayed a little longer."

"Of course." Recalling the films she had seen, an
impulse struck her, one she couldn't deny. "I'd like to have
some fresh air before we leave. Do you mind?"

A smile touched his lips. "As you like." He led her
through an open door to a terrace where they were alone.

His arms around her felt so natural, and she longed for
more. "Would you like to kiss me now?"

Bertrand's eyes crinkled with a broader smile. "With
delight."

The touch of lips on hers was sweeter than any dessert

she'd ever had, and she felt her body's thrilling response. They kissed again—a little longer and even sweeter.

Finally, he pulled back, peppering kisses on her shoulder. "I've been waiting for you to know what you wanted. I hope tonight has changed your mind—even a little."

Ginger considered that, weighing messages zinging between her brain and her heart, which were surprisingly in alignment. "It has. I would like to spend more time with you now."

Tightening his embrace, he said, "You've always struck me as a woman who knows what she wants. You're direct, intelligent, and more beautiful than you realize. You're a unique, stunning young woman."

His eyes shimmering, he drew a breath. "I must leave for my assignment in Paris soon. Would you accompany me as my wife? I can promise you the most delicious life imaginable. And plenty of opportunities to continue your studies."

This was the most marvelous idea she'd ever heard. She caressed Bertrand's smooth face and kissed him again. "Let's have a grand adventure together."

## 7

*M*arina lined up serving dishes on a table just outside the cafe kitchen. While she could have hosted the birthday party at the home she and Jack shared, she thought Heather, Ethan, and their friends would enjoy the beach setting more. She had closed the cafe a little early for the evening. This time of year, the tourist traffic declined, and many residents ate early.

She added another plate of skewered vegetables with roasted chicken and pork and placed it beside the vegetable and cheese plates. She glanced at her sister. "Kai, would you put out more napkins?"

"Sure. This is a finger food kind of beach crowd." Kai glanced at the cupcake tower they had constructed. "This idea was much better than a cake."

"I was afraid it might look like a kid's birthday party, but they're still not too old for cupcakes." Leo and Samantha had sneaked two treats early, but Marina had plenty to replenish.

"Not when they're red velvet, carrot cake, and double chocolate. Yum."

"Those are Heather and Ethan's favorites."

"Mine, too." Kai grinned. "Did I tell you I'm eating for two?"

Marina laughed. "Try eating for three. I was huge."

"Does it seem like it was that long ago?"

"When they were little, I hardly had time to do anything except work and look after them. I didn't slow down until they left for university. Only when I stopped being a woman in perpetual motion did I realize how fast the years had flown."

Marina looked for Heather and Ethan in the crowd of young people. They were surrounded by friends and family. Everyone was laughing and having a good time.

Kai nodded toward Heather and Blake. "They sure have become close. I wonder where that's going."

Marina shrugged, thinking about the talk she'd had with Blake about Heather. "They're in love. What can I say?"

"Everyone has to suffer their first love, I suppose."

"Blake seems like a good guy." Even if his parents seemed a little stand-offish, she thought. She had invited them, but they hadn't arrived. It was late now, so maybe something had come up. She bumped Kai's shoulder. "I was Heather's age when I married Stan."

"You were really young." Kai raised her brow. "Don't you want her to wait?"

"They're adults. What I want doesn't matter anymore." Marina might have influence, but the twins were making their own decisions now. "I've learned I have little control over who they decide to date."

Kai laughed. "Unless they're lunatics or something."

Brooke came up behind them and threw her arms around her sisters. "Are you talking about my boys again?"

"Hey, you," Kai said. "How's the newest one?"

"She's pretty calm," Brooke replied. "I think I'll have to wake her up to give birth. I only hope she can sleep through the male ruckus in my house. But I'm thrilled to be having a girl at last. It will still be two against four, but at least I won't be alone anymore."

"I'm so happy for you," Marina said, hugging her. "How is Chip taking this?"

Brooke glanced at her husband, who was talking to Jack and Axe. "At first, we were both shocked, but now he's going all out in a blaze of Barbie pink."

"Axe bought a miniature pink tool kit," Kai said. "And I don't mean the toy kind. I didn't even get that."

"Keep that away from her for a few years," Brooke said, chuckling. "How have you been feeling?"

Kai twisted her lips to one side. "A little better, although I've had some weird stuff going on. Being pregnant is like some alien being taking over your body. Not to mention stretching it into a new shape I've never seen before. We can talk later. I don't want to ruin this vibe."

"Have you been feeling bad?" Marina shot a look of concern at Brooke.

"The morning sickness has passed, but I'm not sure how I'm supposed to feel now," Kai replied, biting her lip. "I've never done this before."

"You're probably fine." Brooke rubbed Kai's arm. "But I'll go with you to the doctor if you want."

"I'd like that," Kai said, sounding relieved. "This is when you really wish you had a mother, not to minimize Ginger in any way. It's just been a long time since she had a baby."

"We understand," Marina said, trading another look with Brooke. "We're both here for you."

Kai swallowed hard and hugged her. "I don't know what I'd do without you two."

"Fortunately, you won't have to," Marina said, smiling. She remembered being scared with the twins. That was twenty-two years ago tonight, and Ginger had been her rock.

Leo tugged on her sleeve. "Hey, Marina. Dad said to ask you when you're going to light the candles. I think he wants a cupcake."

"Let's light them now." He had helped her put candles on the cake. "Would you tell Heather and Ethan we're ready?"

"Okay." He set off with his friend Samantha beside him.

"Help me light the candles," Marina said to Brooke, handing her a lighter.

Presently, Heather appeared, dragging Ethan behind her. "Gosh, you act like I'm torturing you. Just blow out your share of the candles. You win a couple of tournaments and suddenly, you're too good for this?"

"I never said that. I was right in the middle of telling a story." Ethan threw up his hands at the sight of the candles.

"What the heck? How many candles did you use, Mom? This looks like a bonfire."

Leo piped up, showing his stepbrother his handiwork. "That's your side, Ethan. You got the blue candles, and Heather has the pink candles. So you each have your own now. No more sharing."

"Well, I guess that makes sense," Ethan said, tousling Leo's hair.

Ginger started singing the birthday song, and everyone joined in.

Marina watched her twins' eyes sparkle with happiness as the raucous chorus rang out. The last few years had been a transition for them, but at last, they were both in good places in their lives.

After dropping out of Duke, Ethan was proving himself in the amateur golf circuit and planning to turn pro, and Heather was graduating and entertaining job offers.

As the song ended, Ginger said, "Make a wish, and aim high."

Ethan shot his sister a mischievous look before they leaned forward. Heather blew out hers with a long breath, while Ethan needed a couple of attempts, thanks to his exaggerated cheek-puffing shenanigans. Laughter exploded around them as the last candle flickered out.

"What kind are these?" asked the athletic young woman who had come with Ethan. "They all look so yummy."

Marina reeled off the choices again. "Take a couple," she added. Ethan told her they had met golfing, and she seemed nice enough.

A murmur of satisfaction rippled through the crowd as

Heather's friends and Ethan's golfing buddies swarmed the cupcakes and began to eat.

Heather handed one to her boyfriend. "Saved you a double chocolate one. These are the best."

Blake shook his head. "Thanks, but I can't eat right now."

"Are you feeling okay, sweetie?" Heather asked, furrowing her brow. "You didn't have much for dinner either."

"I'm okay." Blake checked the time. "But there's something I need to talk to you about. Could you come with me?"

"Sure," Heather replied, looking curious and a little concerned.

Marina watched Blake lead Heather toward the fire pit at the edge of the patio. Her heart leapt for them. She'd been watching them all evening.

"Hey, Marina," Kai began.

"Shh, not now." Marina waved a hand.

"What's going on?" Kai followed her line of sight.

Brooke and Ginger leaned in, too. Marina motioned to Jack and pressed a finger to her lips. *This is it.* This was the moment she'd been waiting for.

With the firelight illuminating their silhouettes, Blake dropped to one knee and brought a ring from his pocket. Before he could finish, Heather nodded her ecstatic answer, pulled him up, and flung her arms around him, screaming with joy.

"I think that's a yes," Jack said, chuckling. "That sure was easier than the way we did it."

Marina poked him in the ribs. "Took you long enough, but I wouldn't have had it any other way."

When Blake scooped Heather up and whirled her around, their friends cheered them on.

Blinking back tears of joy, Marina pressed a hand to her heart. "I'm so happy for them." Blake had asked her permission, which Marina thought was sweet, even if it was a little old-fashioned. But she liked that about him. He was solid and, in some ways, even reminded her of Stan. Her first husband had loved being out on the ocean, too.

Ethan was the first to congratulate them, hugging them both at the same time.

"Those three get along so well," Marina said.

She hoped Ethan would find someone Heather liked, too. Maybe it would be the young woman he'd brought tonight, although they didn't seem that serious about each other.

After the congratulations, Heather raced toward her with tears of happiness on her cheeks. "Mom, we're engaged!" She held out a glittering diamond solitaire on her finger. "Blake told me he asked you first."

"I'm so happy for you, honey." Wiping away tears of her own, she hugged Heather and then embraced Blake, who was going to be part of the family. "I didn't know when it would happen, though. I was dying to tell you, but Blake swore me to secrecy."

"Thanks for keeping the secret," he said, his face shining with happiness. "I'd planned to propose at Christmas, but I couldn't wait. As soon as I bought the ring, I wanted to give it to her."

"You'll make a fine couple," Ginger said. "You have my blessing, too. Now we have an engagement party to plan."

Heather and Blake exchanged a look of excitement. "We'd love that," Heather said.

"Then it's settled." Ginger clasped her hands. "We have so much to do. And Marina, you and Jack must meet Blake's parents."

"I'm looking forward to it," Marina said, taking her husband's hand. But as she did, she caught a glimpse of Blake. A look of concern flashed across his face before turning back to Heather.

Although Marina didn't say anything that might spoil the moment, she wondered if Blake's parents were as pleased as they were. Yet, Heather was sweet, intelligent, lovely, talented, and kind. And she adored Blake. Any in-laws would be happy to have Heather as a new daughter-in-law.

Surely, she'd imagined Blake's reaction. She turned to him. "I'll call your parents and introduce ourselves."

Before Blake could reply, he and Heather were drawn into their crowd of friends. Marina dabbed her eyes and watched them go.

Ginger put her arm around Marina's shoulder. "Heather has chosen well, and she'll soon start a new chapter in her life. How exciting for her. I hope she's as happy as I was with Bertrand. Why, I still remember every moment of that happy day."

Jack leaned toward her. "I'm looking forward to hearing all about it."

Smiling, Ginger tapped his cheek. "You will, my dear. You will."

Marina gazed around the patio, fixing the scene in her mind. Her little girl was grown and would soon move out of Ginger's cottage to join Blake and make a home with him. They would most likely remain in Summer Beach. Her mind skipped ahead to grandchildren, a possibility that seemed so far away.

But for now, she had an engagement party to plan and her daughter's future in-laws to meet.

# 8

The late afternoon sun slanted through the little whitewashed chapel in Summer Beach, bathing the vestibule in a golden glow. Ginger's simple, bias-cut candlelight gown shimmered like spun sugar.

She waited in the entrance room with her mother while her father parked the car on the narrow street. The ocean breeze from an open window cooled the small area.

"You look breathtaking, my dear." Her mother's eyes shone with unshed tears of happiness.

Ginger beamed, though she recalled her mother had always dreamed of making a wedding dress for her. "You're sure you don't mind that my dress is store-bought?"

Mary Lou kissed her daughter's cheek. "This is your new life. It's right that Bertrand bought your dress so that you'd look how he wanted you to on your wedding day."

Her mother's words stung a little. "It's the modern way, Mama. He said he loves me in anything I wear, so I choose clothes to suit me and the situation. It's quite efficient."

"You always were so bright and practical." Her mother blinked back tears. "I'm just happy you're marrying a man you love."

"Because of your efforts and support," Ginger said, wiping a tear from her mother's cheek. "Wherever I am, I promise I'll write often with every detail, so you'll feel like you're there with me."

Since being out in the world, Ginger had observed her social surroundings with the eye of a scientist. For all her mother's instructions about making the most of her intellectual gifts and choosing a husband Ginger wanted, Mary Lou Sheraton was still mired in old-fashioned roles in her marriage.

However, Ginger couldn't blame her mother entirely; that was her father's *modus operandi*, and her mother chose to accept the status quo to keep the peace.

Ginger smoothed a hand across the silk dress. She loved the cut and quality of the fine clothing she'd discovered in New York that was as well-crafted as what she and her mother could make. Of course, the cost reflected that, but it didn't faze Bertrand. Over her dress, she wore a long, delicate lace coat that brushed her satin pumps.

With her heels, she was nearly as tall as her husband to be. *I like that we're on an equal footing,* he'd said when they'd danced on their first date. She'd loved hearing that.

The chatter of guests filtered through the closed door. It was almost time.

Her small bouquet of ivory roses from her mother's garden released a soft scent, calming her nerves with every breath.

"I can hardly believe you're moving so far away." Mary

Lou hesitated, wiping tears gathering in the corner of her eye. She adjusted Ginger's strand of pearls—another gift from Bertrand. "You're a vision in this gown; he can't deny that."

This realization of their move was dawning on Ginger, too. An uncharacteristic lump rose in her throat at the raw emotion in her mother's voice, so she glanced down at her dress again, her mind racing to the familiar. "This bias-cut drape is doubtless a result of mathematical precision in the cut. It's a study in geometry."

Mary Lou laughed and pulled her daughter into an embrace. "Leave it to you to deconstruct the poetry of a wedding gown into pure mathematics." She cupped Ginger's face in her palms. "My brilliant, practical girl. I'm so proud of the remarkable woman you've become. Bertrand is a lucky man."

At the mention of her soon-to-be husband's name, Ginger's chest constricted with excitement. Taking a steadying breath, she turned toward the doorway separating her from the man she loved.

Organ music filled the air, and Ginger could feel the vibration through the floorboards.

Her father stepped inside, looking ill at ease in his suit. "If that man doesn't take good care of you in Paris, you're to come straight home, you hear?"

"Why, Stu, that isn't like you at all," Mary Lou said with surprise.

He gave a self-conscious shrug. "Things change."

Beneath her father's scowl, she saw pride and love in his expression.

Blinking hard, Stu took her hand and squeezed it. "I don't want to lose you to Paris, that's all."

"I'll be back, Pa."

"And probably with babies," Mary Lou added. "We love you, darling. We'll miss you, that's all."

"Me, too." She kissed her father's cheek. "I'm ready now."

Ginger slid her hand through the crook in his elbow as he opened the door. Her mother also held her arm. This was how Ginger wanted it.

Their guests turned and, with a murmur of surprise, stood beaming as she entered between her mother and father.

The sight of Bertrand awaiting her at the end of the aisle stole Ginger's breath for a moment. His tailored suit accentuated the lean strength of his frame and erect posture. His gray eyes, filled with adoration, anchored her in a way her rational mind could never quite quantify.

With his gaze trained on her, Bertrand mouthed the words, *I love you.*

She smiled, still amazed that she had fallen in love so quickly these past few whirlwind weeks. Yet, she also felt like she was marrying her best friend. Since meeting, she had shared all her dreams and aspirations with him. They had grown to know each other long before their first date at the ambassador's estate.

Ever since that evening, they had been nearly inseparable, dining together every day he was in town.

Bertrand's face shone with such admiration and devotion. How had she not detected his true feelings for so long? When she'd confided that in him, he had laughed and said it was only because she thought more with her head than her heart.

Fortunately, he loved that about her, though he promised to make sure she learned the heart was just as important.

Now, Ginger couldn't imagine ever being without him again. Love was changing her; she could feel it, even if she couldn't explain it. With her horizons broadening, she noticed more beauty in the world, more possibilities.

At last, Ginger stood before the man she loved, and her parents took their seats. Bertrand's smile was warm and reassuring.

The minister began, and Ginger felt as if she were floating in the rafters, watching the scene from above. Her parents sat in the first row, beaming with pride. They looked happier than she could ever recall seeing them. Her brothers and childhood friends filled the other pews, some with dates, others with new spouses: Sylvia, Pearl, and Juanita. Her friends Helen and Chase, who married last year, were there, and Helen was already pregnant.

On the other side sat Kurt Powell and his wife. Kurt hated to lose Ginger, but he was happy for Bertrand, his closest friend. Kurt's younger brother had also driven with them; Oliver was about Ginger's age. The three handsome men were the life of any party they attended.

The brief ceremony passed by in a blur. Ginger couldn't keep the radiant smile from her face as they exchanged rings. As she clasped her husband's hands and the minister pronounced them husband and wife, happiness washed over her.

"At last, my love," Bertrand murmured, taking her in his arms.

"At last, and forever," she whispered, gliding on a wave of love so consuming that it rendered the world around them small and insignificant.

They sealed their vow with a sweet kiss and the promise of much more to come.

After greeting and mingling with their guests, her mother hugged her. "We'll leave for the house and have everyone follow us now. You two take your time." She beamed at Bertrand and kissed Ginger on the cheek.

Her parents were hosting a reception and dinner at their home. Her mother had been cooking and baking for days before Ginger and Bertrand arrived.

"We're ready now," Ginger said.

"Wait," Bertrand said in a husky voice, taking her hand. "We'll follow them shortly. Let's take a moment to ourselves."

They stepped into the adjoining wisteria-draped court-yard and sat on a stone bench, releasing the tension they'd built up. They both drew in deep breaths and rested in each other's embrace.

"Right before the ceremony, I received a call about Paris," Bertrand said, kissing her shoulder. "Our application for the furnished flat was approved, so it will be ready for us when we arrive."

"That's wonderful, darling. What a relief." They would have a week before they left. It hardly seemed real to her.

"Marie and her mother will help you get anything you need. Most of the wives are good friends. Of course,

Marie's mother is a French citizen, so she knows all the best shops. That will be a real advantage to you."

"When will I be able to visit my parents?" she asked, knowing how much her mother would miss her.

"We'll return together twice a year," he replied, smoothing her hair. "They're my family, too."

She knew this was important to Bertrand. As much as he'd loved his parents, they were no longer with him. He had a strong desire to recreate a family. Kurt was like a brother to him, and he treated her parents as his own.

They talked a little more until Bertrand kissed her and said, "I have something else to show you now. Are you ready?"

She twisted the diamond band that rested on her finger. "Everything is perfect. What else could I possibly want?"

"One final surprise." His eyes sparkling with mischief, he rose. "I think you'll like this one." He gestured down a winding path that led toward the beach. "This way, darling."

Bemused, she followed him. They strolled a short distance before he stopped.

Nestled near the beach against a backdrop of bluffs and lapping waves stood a white, two-story cottage. Wildflowers and bougainvillea bloomed around it in fuchsia and purple.

"This home is my wedding gift to you." His lips curved into the mysterious smile she loved. "No matter where we roam, I want you to have a home we can return to and root our family." He swept an arm out to encompass the stunning panorama. "Summer Beach will always be that."

Tears filled Ginger's eyes as she flung her arms around him. "It's everything I could have wanted." Her head spinning with delight, Ginger showered him with kisses. "How did you manage this?"

"Your parents are quite good at keeping secrets, I found. Welcome home, my dear. It's yours to decorate."

Ginger's gaze drifted over the house, her keen aesthetic eye evaluating the possibilities. Beyond the cottage, fiery coral hues streaked across the evening sky.

An idea bloomed in her mind. "Let's paint it."

"Whatever you like. What color do you imagine?"

She lifted her face toward the sunset. "That gorgeous coral shade. Isn't it magnificent?"

"Anything you want." Bertrand laughed. "We'll call it the Coral Cottage."

Ginger smiled with delight. Since she'd left home, her orderly world had shifted beyond what she ever could have imagined. In her soul, she sensed a marvelous adventure unfolding.

This cottage would be their refuge. Feeling safe, she could fully surrender to the glorious unknown.

Bertrand opened the door to reveal a foyer bathed in the rosy glow of flickering candles. But it was the vision beyond that made Ginger smile: A table laden with crystal glasses and a vase of her mother's roses, set for what appeared to be a celebratory feast.

Realization dawned on her, and she turned to Bertrand. "You're a sly character."

"We'll stay here tonight." He waggled his eyebrows mischievously before scooping her into his arms and crossing the threshold.

Once he did, their family and friends materialized from hiding, beaming and applauding the newlyweds.

As Bertrand set Ginger on her feet, she turned, taking in every detail. Her father appeared carrying champagne.

"For my daughter and my new son," he said proudly.

Tears of joy trickled down Ginger's cheeks as she embraced her father's sturdy frame. "Thank you, Pa." He'd finally come around.

Mary Lou joined her husband in a toast to them. "May your lives be an adventure, and may you embrace it with the same passion you've embraced this day. Welcome to the family, dear Bertrand."

"Thank you from the depths of my heart," he said, raising his glass to them.

With a confident smile, Ginger tapped her glass to Bertrand's and their journey ahead. "To our future," she echoed, daring to dream.

## 9

The hum of cocktail conversations and the glow of chandeliers at the ambassador's soiree filled Ginger's senses. Their social life in Paris was active due to Bertrand's calendar filled with diplomatic affairs.

"Having a good time?" Bertrand asked.

Ginger squeezed his hand. "Always with you."

He kissed her cheek with a bemused smile that lit her heart. "Come with me. I need to speak with Grant Jones-Smith."

"The way he looks at me makes me uncomfortable. Can you spare me?"

"Of course, darling. Don't judge him too harshly; you are a sight to behold, especially in your wedding ensemble. Only we know what happened that night, don't we?"

Her cheeks warmed at his words. "You're incorrigible." And she loved it. "Go on, have your talk with Grant. I'll watch the room for a bit; it always humors me."

"I won't be too long."

Ginger watched him go. In her eyes, he was easily the most handsome man in the room—or anywhere they went. She nursed a glass of champagne while Bertrand circulated among colleagues.

She had learned how to occupy herself at these functions. For example, she had already tallied the number of guests—one hundred fifty-three. Idly, she calculated the number of crystals in all the chandeliers, which probably rivaled the number of sequins on one woman's mauve evening gown. She had moved on to multiplying the hours likely required to construct each light fixture when a man in an evening suit tapped her crystal glass with a resounding ring.

A playful smirk danced on his lips. "You look bored beyond belief."

He had an American accent. East Coast, she imagined. "I'm watching my husband."

"Liar. You were studying those chandeliers as if planning a heist and estimating their worth."

"That depends on the cost of each piece of crystal." Ginger named the number she'd calculated, give or take a few missing pieces. "If you know that, I can give you a fairly accurate assessment. I can share that calculation if you have time."

Instead of excusing himself then, as most men would have done at this point, he stared at her. "Are you serious?"

"I've met sixty-three-and-a-half people this evening, though my husband is much better at names than numbers. I prefer this." She glanced up again, giving him another chance to leave.

Amusement crinkled his eyes. "A half?"

"Half of who they might be." She sniffed at the waste of human potential. The vacuous, the bored, or those who had given up on life. What a shame, she thought.

"Quite right," he replied, looking slightly awed. "And who is your husband?"

"Bertrand Delavie."

The man's eyebrows raised. "Why, you don't say?"

"That's exactly what I said." Ginger wondered why people said such things.

She turned her gaze upward again, signaling her disinterest. Perhaps he would leave to converse with her husband, who was much more affable.

"Are you appraising the chandeliers?"

"No, but I would place the value at..." She quickly named a figure, to his apparent surprise.

Seemingly intrigued, he inclined his head. "Sounds like a good guess."

"I don't guess. That's for amateurs." Slightly annoyed, she went on. "Lacking specific information on value, I assumed each crystal is worth four U.S. dollars. If it were six dollars, you'd increase that by fifty percent. Value is a variable to be confirmed."

He lifted a corner of his mouth in a half grin. "How about that in French francs?"

"Of course, one moment. The prevailing exchange rate is..."

The man looked on in amazement as Ginger rattled off numbers in two currencies and then multiplied that by the number of chandeliers in the room. This was a cheap parlor trick, but it kept her mind occupied.

"What if you knew the cost?"

"Helpful, though cost and value are different."

"You could add percentages for the cost of labor and profit. Realizing that these are only assumptions." A smile touched his lips as if amused.

"Alright." Without having anything more worthwhile to do, she spun out a few more numbers before turning back to him. After finishing, she waited for him to leave. They always did.

When he didn't, she asked, "Shouldn't you be moving on to someone more important or fascinating? I'm only a career diplomat's wife."

He shook his head in amazement. "I've never seen anyone do math in their head like that."

"I'm sure any college professor of mathematics could do the same. Though I wouldn't know." Without higher education in mathematics or better fluency in French, she hadn't been able to further her study in Paris, although she was working on the latter.

Bertrand caught her eye and touched his lips as though in thought. She smiled and did the same.

They'd developed little signals they used at functions. A finger touch to the lips meant *I love you*. A sweep of a finger to an eyebrow signaled the desire to leave; a tap to the forehead meant *yes*, and a touch of the chin for *no*. Fingers to the chest meant *come here, I need you*.

"I'm not sure even a professor would have your rapid mental dexterity," the man continued. He stared at her with a look of disbelief creasing his brow.

"I didn't catch your name," Ginger said, extending her hand.

"Forgive me," he said. "Silas Rutherford. And what do you do with your time here in Paris?"

Back to trite conversation, she thought with a small sigh. "Study French, math, and science."

"That's quite aggressive. No shopping?"

"I didn't say that." He showed no sign of leaving. "And I read."

Silas inclined his head. "What do you enjoy reading?"

"Mathematical theories, scientific discoveries, puzzle solving techniques." From experience, she'd learned that response was often met with blank looks.

Silas stared at her again.

Just then, a woman approached them looking perturbed. Ginger assumed this was his wife.

Silas fluttered a hand to the woman. Perhaps he was late delivering her promised cocktail. "I should like to continue this conversation, but I've overstayed my welcome. Would you excuse me?"

"Delighted," she replied, turning a bright smile his way. "To have met you, of course," she quickly added. She was, after all, a diplomat's wife. Bertrand expected cordiality of her, even as he secretly agreed with her assessments.

GINGER BREEZED into Bertrand's study the following week, surprised to find him deep in conversation with the man she'd spoken to at the party. *Silas Rutherford.* An undercurrent of tension rippled between the two men, piquing her curiosity.

"Your wife is truly remarkable, Bertrand," Silas said as she approached. "Her mental acuity is astonishing."

While Ginger enjoyed the recognition, she also noted the pinched look around Bertrand's eyes. What had him so ill at ease?

"Her skills would be invaluable to our intelligence efforts," Silas stated. "I want to recruit her."

The words hung in the air, practically shimmering with unspoken possibility. Ginger's mind began to whir, with visions of coded dispatches and clandestine operations dancing in her thoughts. To assist in such vital, high-stakes work would be the grandest mental exercise she could conceive.

"You know the dangers of such work, Silas." Bertrand's commanding baritone sliced through her reverie. "I cannot allow Ginger to be put in harm's way."

"Forgive me, but we need her skills. There aren't many—"

"Ginger." Bertrand spied her and rose from his desk. "I didn't see you there. You remember Mr. Rutherford?"

"Silas, please." The man was quick to extend his hand without waiting for her to offer hers.

That small action was sure to annoy Bertrand. "Of course. We solved mathematical problems for a little while."

Bertrand looked confused. "About what?"

When she hesitated, Silas jumped in with an answer. "The number of crystals in the chandelier and their value in U.S. dollars and French francs, and various cost and profit margin calculations. It was truly remarkable."

"Parlor games," Ginger added with a self-conscious

shrug. She hadn't meant for Bertrand to know how bored she was.

He nodded slowly. "So that's how you amuse yourself when I leave you alone." After a slight hesitation, he turned to Silas. "I'm not making any promises, but I will speak to my wife about your proposal."

Silas inclined his head in appreciation. "Of course. Take your time. But I urge you not to immediately disregard the opportunity before her. We need people like her."

THAT EVENING, after their housekeeper had cleared the dinner dishes from the table, Bertrand took her hand. "I've always known you have a brilliant mind meant for great discoveries. How would you like to put it to work?"

Ginger's eyes lit up like the Parisian night. "Do you mean Silas's offer?"

Bertrand nodded and explained the other man's proposition. "You need to understand the dangers, my dear."

"And the potential to save countless lives. Using my skills to make a difference is what I've longed to do."

"I'm aware of that." He took out his pipe and tapped it in his hand as he spoke. The scent of his vanilla tobacco sweetened the air. "On the surface, it's high-level study, but if certain characters discovered what you're doing, it could be dangerous."

Ginger recognized the nervous gesture and the catch in his voice. "I'll be careful."

"You must think about your parents as well."

"And you." Ginger spoke with understanding. "I know the risks, my love. But I also know I cannot sit idly by when

I have the intelligence to help. This is my chance to be part of something greater than myself. For my country and for others."

"Alright, but we must take every precaution." With a sign of surrender, he pulled her close. "This will require travel to Virginia for training. Can you manage on your own?"

"I manage fine when you're away."

"I had to ask. You're my wife, and my job is to protect you."

"You do. But you must also let me go." Ginger's mind was already sizzling with excitement. "I'll come back like a boomerang. I promise."

---

It was a beautiful spring morning when Ginger slipped into a nondescript back door a few blocks from the U.S. embassy in Paris. She was a few minutes late, having raced from an early doctor's appointment.

She was still numb at the diagnosis.

But she had no time to process that. Immediately, she unlocked a cabinet and withdrew her work from the day before. She settled into her chair at the wooden desk and addressed the stack of documents.

The room fairly hummed with the quiet concentration of a handful of other cryptologists, each bent over their work. Though she'd only been at this for a few months, Ginger felt as if she'd finally found her true calling.

She was skilled at pattern recognition, the initial step in decoding messages. To an outsider, the work might seem monotonous, even mind-numbing. But to Ginger, each new coded message was an exhilarating challenge, a complex equation taunting her—yet, destined to be unraveled.

As she reached for her first document of the day, a shadow fell across her desk. Looking up, she met the approving gaze of her supervisor, Reginald Thompson.

"Mrs. Delavie," he said in a low voice, mindful of the quiet room. "A moment of your time, please."

Ginger nodded, rising to follow him to his office. Curious glances from her colleagues also followed her. Her unique position as both a skilled cryptologist and the wife of a high-ranking man in diplomatic services hadn't gone unnoticed.

Once inside Reginald's office, he gestured for her to take a seat.

"I'm sorry for being a few minutes late," she began.

"That's not why I called you in," he said, lacing his fingers on the desk. "Your work has been exemplary. The patterns you've identified in Eastern European communications have provided invaluable insights. And saved lives."

A warm glow blossomed in Ginger's chest. "Thank you, sir. I'm grateful for the opportunity to contribute."

Thompson's lips quirked in a rare smile. "Which is why I'm recommending you for more advanced training in Virginia. Six weeks, this time. Starting next month. You'll work with top analysts on more sensitive materials."

Ginger's heart raced with excitement. Advanced training meant more complex codes, higher stakes, and the chance to improve sensitive situations. But a small voice in the back of her mind whispered a reminder.

"That might not be a good time."

Thompson continued, "You have a unique situation, Mrs. Delavie. We'll make any necessary accommodations. Your husband's position affords you certain flexibilities."

She bristled slightly at the implication she received special treatment, but practicality won out over pride.

"May I let you know tomorrow?"

He nodded, satisfied.

Settling back into her chair, Ginger picked up another document with renewed vigor. A profound sense of purpose washed over her.

Each pattern she identified, each code she cracked, led to something greater. She was no longer just Mrs. Bertrand Delavie, the nameless extension of her husband. In this room, she was a vital cog in the machinery of national security, using her intelligence to protect her country and her family.

Yet, sooner or later, she would have to address what would soon become obvious.

## 10

*M*arina couldn't remember when she had seen Heather so happy. Her daughter's face glowed as she talked about her plans with Blake for the future. She had stopped by Marina's house to borrow a cocktail dress for a party that one of Blake's nonprofit rescue organization supporters was having.

Heather held up the black dress. "This is perfect. Everything I have is too young and too short. I want to make a good impression."

Her daughter was maturing into a lovely young woman. "Take some heels to match."

"Thanks," Heather replied as she selected a pair. "I want you to know that Blake and I have made some important decisions."

"Already?" Marina sat on the bench at the foot of her bed. "It's only been a couple of days."

"I know, but we have so much to do," Heather replied, joining her. "I've turned down my out-of-town job offers, so

I'm staying in Summer Beach. That's obvious now, I guess."

Marina thought that was a good idea. "Do you know what you want to do here? Of course, you're welcome to continue working at the cafe, but I thought you wanted more of a challenge in marketing."

Heather grinned. "How about helping you run the food truck side of the business? I know you want to expand that, and I have a lot of ideas to appeal to the new communities we go into. Videos, social media, mailing lists. And an entire branding campaign. You're going to need that, Mom."

"I could use your help with all of that," Marina said thoughtfully.

"And the cookbook will be an important part of the campaign."

"Will you have time for that?"

"I'll make time," Heather said. "I'm so excited about all of this. In one of my marketing classes, we had a case study about how a company grew through branding, which made their franchise program one of the most popular."

They talked a little more while Marina let Heather select jewelry to match the dress. She tucked a necklace and bracelet into a small pouch and gave that to her daughter. "Did you and Blake talk about where you plan to live?"

"I'll move into his house after the wedding. But we want to buy a home of our own soon." Heather hugged her. "I still need to study tonight, so I should go back to Ginger's."

"Before I forget, did Blake give you his parents' number?"

"Oh, sure," Heather replied, taking out her phone. "I'll send it to you. See you later."

As Marina watched her go, her heart was full for her daughter's good fortune. Finding someone to love wasn't easy, but she and Blake were a good match.

MARINA STOOD at the kitchen window the next morning, her fingers absently tracing the rim of her coffee mug. She set aside her concerns over Blake's parents not attending Heather's party. Blake had also invited them, and she wondered if he was disappointed that they weren't there for the engagement.

She understood that people were busy, and it was almost an hour's drive from their home. Perhaps if he'd told them, they would have made the trip for him. Still, they would all have many happy occasions ahead.

Marina picked up her phone and tapped the number Heather had given her for Blake's parents. The line rang twice before a woman's voice answered.

"Hello, Arlette? This is Marina, Heather's mother," she said, injecting warmth into her voice.

"Oh, yes," Arlette said, sounding slightly distant.

Nevertheless, Marina continued, "My husband, Jack, and I want to invite you and Ken to our home for dinner. Now that our children are engaged, we're looking forward to meeting you."

There was a pause on the other end of the line, long enough for Marina to wonder if the connection had been lost.

"Arlette? Are you still there?"

"Yes, I'm here." Arlette's voice sounded oddly strained. "I suppose we should meet in person."

Marina forged ahead, determined to bridge the unexpected coolness. "We're planning an engagement party. I would love your input and will be happy to invite guests you want to attend. When would you like—"

"This week," Arlette interrupted. "We should meet this week. There's a cafe in Orange County. The Bluebird. Are you free Thursday evening?"

Taken aback by the abruptness, Marina agreed to the meeting. As she hung up, a knot of unease formed in her stomach. Something didn't seem right. Or maybe she'd reached Arlette at the wrong time.

THE BLUEBIRD CAFE was a quaint spot with pale blue walls and crisp white tablecloths. Marina and Jack arrived early, the bell above the door chiming as they entered. The aroma of freshly baked bread filled the air, but it did little to soothe Marina's growing apprehension.

"Relax," Jack said. "Maybe she was having a bad day."

"I hope that's all it was." Marina chewed her lip while they waited.

A large, expensive-looking car pulled up in front of the restaurant, and a well-dressed couple got out.

"That man looks like Blake," Jack said. "I'll bet that's Ken and Arlette Hayes. In a new Rolls-Royce, no less. I'm surprised they didn't suggest a more exclusive restaurant."

"Maybe they're being modest."

"By driving that?"

Marina had to concede that point.

When the couple walked in, they introduced themselves. Marina sensed tension in their tight faces, even though they shook hands and were polite enough.

Arlette wore one of the largest wedding rings Marina had ever seen outside *People* magazine. Marina wasn't staring, but it was hard to miss. Her husband had another diamond ring unlike anything she'd ever seen on a man. Knowing Blake and how practical he was, she wouldn't have guessed his parents were like this.

As they settled into their seats, Marina began the conversation. "We're so glad to meet you. Blake is such a wonderful young man, and we're delighted that he and Heather are such a good match."

Before anyone could respond, a waitress approached with menus. Ken waved her off without accepting the menus. "Give us a few minutes," he said in a gruff tone.

That wasn't a good sign. Marina's heart sank as Ken leaned forward, his expression grave.

"I'm sure your Heather is a lovely girl." His words were clearly patronizing. "And maybe Blake has been sowing some wild oats in Summer Beach. But my son has been engaged to another young woman for several years. She's a family friend, someone he's known since childhood."

The words hit Marina like a physical blow. She glanced at Jack, seeing her shock mirrored in his eyes.

"My daughter is not some wild oats, some fling..." Marina was so upset she stumbled over her words. Jack rested a reassuring hand on her thigh.

Arlette spoke up, her cheeks flushed with embarrassment. "I'm sorry you drove all this way, but I didn't want to tell you this over the phone."

Her husband nodded. "We have nothing else to talk about. This engagement to your daughter is off."

Marina found her voice, anger rising to replace her initial shock. "They are adults, and that decision is up to Blake. He proposed to Heather at her birthday party with a beautiful ring he'd picked out for her. The one we invited you to."

Arlette looked away, clearly uncomfortable.

Ken shrugged. "Our son can be impulsive."

"Blake appears to know what he wants," Jack said, trying a reasonable approach. "He and Heather have been together for quite some time now."

Ken's face hardened. "We're not going to argue about this. It's unfortunate that your daughter will be disappointed, but that's Blake's doing, not ours."

"Unfortunate?" Marina couldn't believe his cavalier tone. "This isn't some high school crush. They're in love and are making plans. Heather has turned down job offers to stay in Summer Beach."

"Again, we're terribly sorry," Arlette said, averting her eyes.

"It really is their decision," Jack added. "Blake is committed to Heather, and they want to marry as soon as she graduates from university."

Ken lowered his voice. "She's not pregnant, is she? Because if she's entrapped our son, she shouldn't expect any money out of the deal."

Arlette looked horrified. "That wasn't necessary," she whispered to her husband.

"We have to know, don't we?" Ken's tone was rude and insinuating.

"That's it." Marina couldn't take this any longer. She stood abruptly, her chair scraping loudly against the floor. The few other patrons turned to look, but she hardly noticed. "My daughter," she said, her voice low and fierce, "did not entrap your son. How dare you suggest such a thing?"

She grabbed her purse, her hands shaking with anger. "Jack, we're leaving. I won't sit here and listen to that man insult my daughter."

"You haven't heard the last of this," Jack said to Ken. He wrapped his arm around Marina and led her from the restaurant.

As he helped her into his VW van, tears of frustration pricked Marina's eyes. Her heart was breaking for her daughter. "What are we going to tell Heather?"

"Let me talk to Blake first." Jack sighed heavily. "Something doesn't seem right. I don't think Arlette wants to support her husband in this. Ken might be threatening to cut Blake out of an inheritance or something."

"He appears to be self-supporting, though."

"I don't know. Family dynamics can be awfully strange."

Marina nodded, steeling herself for the conversation ahead. As they drove back to Summer Beach on empty stomachs, she was saddened to think how quickly their joy had turned to heartache. And more pressingly, what would Blake have to say about this?

## 11

*G*inger motioned to her great-granddaughter as she skirted between tables at the cafe. "Heather, dear, may we have more coffee?" This morning, they were seated at the far end of the patio for privacy.

Heather turned toward them with a dazzling smile. "I'll make a fresh pot for you and leave it here. I know how Jack guzzles his coffee," she added, grinning.

"What a lovely young woman," Ginger said as Heather walked away. "And so happy." In many ways, Heather reminded her of herself when she was young. Smart, determined, and so much in love. She sighed, glad that Heather had met her match. "Oh, to be that age again with a lifetime ahead."

A shadow crossed Jack's face, and he shifted in his chair. "Before we start, I want you to know I'm to meet Blake on his lunch hour today. We might have to cut this session short."

"Not a problem." Ginger detected something odd in his demeanor. "Did you sleep well last night?"

"Got something on my mind, that's all." He flipped open his notebook. "I'll just take notes today. No recording."

"As you wish." She folded her hands, studying him with curiosity. Whatever was bothering him, he wasn't ready to share yet. She could wait.

"So, we've covered your initial meeting with Bertrand and the acquisition of the cottage," Jack began, tapping his pen against his notepad. "But I want to delve deeper into your contributions. Your work during that time was groundbreaking, wasn't it?"

Ginger smiled. "Once again, you're getting ahead of the story. Let me tell it my way."

———

THE BUSTLING ENERGY of Les Deux Magots in *le sixième*, the 6th arrondissement in Paris, hummed around Ginger as she sat at a sidewalk table with Bertrand. One year ago today, she had pledged her life and love to this intriguing man in an intimate ceremony by the sea.

Bertrand brought her hand to his lips, whispering a kiss over her skin. "Happy anniversary, my love," he murmured, his eyes dancing with thoughts she could easily read.

Though they had celebrated earlier that morning with languid lovemaking and decadent breakfast in bed, she still wished to mark the occasion properly.

"Still happy?" he asked.

"Divinely so."

"So am I." He raised his glass to her, "To my exquisite wife. May we celebrate many more anniversaries just like this."

Ginger flushed with pleasure, coupled with a dizzying cocktail of excitement.

"I have some news to share," she began, taking his hands in hers.

Bertrand raised his brow, waiting for her.

She released a breath, feeling flustered despite the many times she had rehearsed this line. "Darling, we're having a child."

For an endless moment, the din of the sidewalk seemed to cease around them. Ginger watched as a rapid progression of shock, elation, and wonderment transformed his features into an expression so exquisite her heart ached.

He finally exhaled; his voice was edged with uncharacteristic huskiness. "A child? You're...we're to be parents?"

She nodded, unable to contain her happiness. "I am, without a doubt, pregnant."

A low, rumbling laugh burst from him, suffused with such joy that he rose from his chair and embraced her, his palms cradling her face as his lips found hers.

"My dearest Ginger," he said when they finally parted, breathless and grinning like adolescents. "What an incredible anniversary gift." His hands slipped lower, spanning her abdomen with reverence. "Imagine, we'll soon greet a little one."

She was nearly as dazed as he was by the enormity of this news. "Are you truly happy? I know the timing isn't quite right given our present circumstances."

Bertrand's expression sobered, though his eyes still

glinted with excitement. "You know I only worry for your safety, *ma chérie*."

"This is why I must continue my work for a while," Ginger insisted, anticipating his next suggestion.

Sure enough, Bertrand's eyes tightened slightly before he pressed on in a placating tone. "It might be best for you to return to Summer Beach."

"No." She placed a finger firmly over his lips, halting the proposal she had known would come. "I will not be coddled away to safety like some fragile flower." Her eyes blazed with ferocious conviction. "This child is precisely why I must work to ensure a better, more secure future. I will not sit idle when I can contribute." In truth, she felt herself on the verge of a momentous discovery, but she needed time.

Her husband's eyes searched hers before he finally shook his head in surrender.

Cupping her face tenderly, he bestowed a lingering kiss upon her lips. "And that's why I adore you, my strong, fierce love. Still, I must insist on a few reasonable precautions. Call your mother and talk all you want. She will be elated."

A trans-Atlantic call was a luxury. "I will. Maybe we could return to Summer Beach just before my due date." That would give her the strong impetus for a breakthrough in her work.

"Consider it planned."

Ginger sighed with happiness. This child was the amazing culmination of the deepest love she had ever known. Her gaze strayed past Bertrand's shoulder, where the sights of her beloved Paris glittered in the sunlight. She smiled, contented now. What better place to have started their family?

"How soon might we return?" Ginger asked, thinking about how much she would miss their life here.

"It's not always my choice. I must go where I'm needed. But we will always return."

---

GINGER LOVED BEING pregnant in Paris. She worked long enough to make significant progress on cracking a code that had long vexed teams of cryptologists, earning her a commendation that she declined.

She didn't want attention drawn to her or her baby, so she insisted the men she worked with take the credit. Still, word spread among their colleagues about what she had accomplished.

At last, it was time to leave; Bertrand received orders for a transfer to Washington, D.C. He worried about her giving birth on the Atlantic crossing or on the train from New York to the West Coast.

They made it to Summer Beach scant weeks before their precious daughter Sandi was born.

While Ginger would miss Paris, this transfer was essential for Bertrand's career. She could continue her work at Arlington Hall. Bertrand found a townhouse for them in Washington, D.C., and they brought an *au pair* from France to help with the baby.

Ginger was pleased that their lives took yet another turn. They attended White House events, saw New York theater productions, and vacationed in Palm Beach. Bertrand taught seminars at universities in Boston, where he reconnected with his old friend Kurt and his brother Oliver. Ginger was delighted to see her former boss as well.

"You must meet some good friends of mine here in Boston," Kurt told them one day during lunch. "Paul and Julia Child. Like you, they've spent time in Paris and traveled the world. I think you'd all get on quite well."

When they met, Ginger was fascinated by the couple, especially Julia, who had studied at Le Cordon Bleu in Paris. She was making a name for herself, having recently written a book on French cooking. Though younger, Ginger was nearly as tall as Julia, and the pair turned heads when they went out. They loved sharing stories about their time in France. Ginger was also intrigued about Julia's work for the government, although they were careful about what they shared.

The two couples soon became fast friends, and Ginger and Bertrand visited Julia and Paul in Cambridge whenever they were in town.

This drizzly, overcast afternoon, Ginger leaned against the kitchen counter of the Child's comfortable home near Harvard Square, watching Julia expertly slice onions with a practiced hand. The aroma of butter melting in a heavy-bottomed pot filled the air, mingling with herbs and spices. The kitchen was warm and inviting.

"Now, dear, the key to a perfect French onion soup is patience," Julia instructed, her distinctive warble filled with enthusiasm as she outlined the steps. "You must let the onions caramelize slowly. It's a labor of love."

Ginger nodded, absorbing every word. "Like a mathematical equation," she mused. "Layers of complexity, each step precise, the solution gradually revealed as you work through it."

Julia's eyebrows shot up, her face breaking into a delighted grin. "Oh, I do like that analogy. Paul, darling, did you hear that? Ginger's comparing my soup to mathematical equations."

A chuckle came from the corner of the kitchen, where Paul was meticulously measuring ingredients for cocktails with Bertrand. "Well, that certainly fits."

Sitting at a table, Bertrand raised his glass. "To cocktail and culinary success."

"Hear, hear," Ginger said.

Julia guided her through the steps of preparing the roast chicken, explaining each step. "Cooking is a blend of art and science. It involves precision, timing, and combining elements for the best result. So relax, be fearless, and enjoy a glass of wine or a cocktail while you make dinner. You'll be happier for it."

While they talked, Ginger tucked a handful of cooked carrots, celery, parsley, thyme, and lemon slices into the cavity of a trussed chicken she'd massaged with butter. "How is this?" she asked when she finished.

Julia nodded her approval. "Very good. Everything tastes better with enough butter. And how did your soufflés turn out last week?"

"Ginger was busy, so I prepared them," Bertrand said. "My soufflés are the height of diplomatic relations. Fluffy little peacekeepers, they turned out to be."

The conversation flowed to their experiences in Paris as

they sipped their drinks. Ginger loved strolling along the Seine, the city of lights sparkling around her.

"Do you remember that little cafe near the Sorbonne?" Ginger asked Bertrand. "Where we'd spend hours over coffee and croissants?"

"Paul and I had our haunts, too," Julia said, naming their favorite spots.

"And the markets," Paul added. "Julia spent hours examining every vegetable, every cut of meat. It was like watching a general plan a campaign."

"One must start with the finest ingredients available," Julia said, pausing for a sip.

As the evening progressed and the meal came together, Ginger was drawn into her friend's culinary world. The precision, creativity, and sheer joy of crafting something delicious resonated with her analytical mind.

Over dinner, as they savored and devoured what they'd prepared, Julia raised her glass. "As I like to say, people who love to eat are always the best people. You and Bertrand certainly qualify."

Ginger expressed her deep appreciation. "What a marvelous evening. You've sparked a new appreciation for cooking in me."

As they clinked glasses, Ginger knew she'd found a new passion and cherished friends.

Bertrand leaned in for a kiss. "The roasted chicken was delicious."

"I'll be sure to replicate it." She sighed happily.

The evening was equal parts humor, warmth, and intellect—with a main dish of culinary excellence. They lingered over their *crème brûlée* that Julia had finished with a blow torch.

Ginger fixed this pleasant evening in her mind, adding it to her mental snapshots. Often, when her work became tedious, she would take a break and flip through these images. Someday, she would revisit all these joyful moments.

## 12

*G*inger smoothed her hand over her cream linen dress as she arrived at the restaurant overlooking Laguna Beach. The afternoon sun cast a golden glow over the crowd gathered on the beachside patio, their faces a mix of sorrow and celebration.

Nearby, musicians played the jazz music she recalled as Kurt's favorite. He and Oliver and Bertrand often argued over who was better: Miles Davis, Louie Armstrong, or John Coltrane.

*Break the tie, Ginger. Who's your choice?*

She had laughed and replied, *Ella Fitzgerald.*

So many memories, so much fun. Lifting her chin, Ginger searched the gathering for Oliver, wondering how much he'd changed. But then, so had she. Would he recognize her?

She scanned faces as she approached the group, recognizing old friends and colleagues. It had been years since she'd seen many of them, but the years melted away as warm smiles and hugs greeted her.

And there, in the middle of a throng of people, stood Oliver. He turned as if sensing her presence, and his face lit with instant recognition.

"Ginger, darling. You made it." Oliver Powell, Kurt's younger brother, approached with open arms. His silver hair caught the sunlight, and his blue eyes sparkled with genuine warmth. Years of laughter lined his face with character.

"How could I miss this lovely celebration?" Ginger replied, embracing him. "Kurt meant so much to Bertrand and me. How are you?"

"Much better now that you're here," he replied. "My brother lived a full life, didn't he? Ninety years of pushing boundaries and charming everyone he met."

"He certainly did." Ginger nodded as memories of Kurt's infectious enthusiasm for technology and life flooded back. "I remember the day he hired me. He changed the course of my life."

As they chatted, Ginger noticed how distinguished Oliver looked in his navy blazer and crisp white shirt, trousers, and deck shoes. Like his brother, he'd always been attractive, but the years had added a distinguished presence.

The ceremony began with friends and family recalling cherished stories about Kurt, punctuated with laughter. Music drifted across the beach as friends and family shared stories of his brilliance, kindness, and zest for life.

Ginger was swept up in the beautiful tribute to Kurt's life and shared her memories of times she and Kurt traveled to New York on business and later, after she and

126 | JAN MORAN

Bertrand were married, when they would all meet for dinner in Boston.

"I remember your wedding," Oliver said. "Kurt and his wife went, and I tagged along for a beach trip." He chuckled. "You were intoxicatingly beautiful."

Ginger smiled at the memory of that magical day. "And here we are again, back at the beach."

"Yes, aren't we?" Oliver said, holding her gaze.

Others pulled him away, so Ginger circulated, speaking to other old friends and new acquaintances.

The breeze picked up as the sun began to set, washing the sky in vibrant shades of pink and coral. When the music ended, guests began to leave.

"Would you stand with me while people leave?" Oliver asked.

"I'm happy to," she replied, feeling comfortable with him. It felt so natural because many were her friends, too.

While the last guests departed, Ginger lingered beside him, chatting and watching the waves crash against the shoreline. A bittersweet ache filled her chest. So much had changed since those early days in Los Angeles, yet the memories remained vivid. How happy she was that she lived such a good life and did much of what she enjoyed.

Like Kurt and Bertrand.

Oliver's voice broke through her reverie. "How about a glass of bubbly—water, that is? We each have to drive home."

"Perfect, I'm parched," she replied, accepting the glass with a smile. They sat at a table near the beach.

Ginger squeezed lime into her water and sipped. "I've been thinking about Kurt introducing Bertrand and me, those exciting days of new technology, and the parties at your family's house in Boston where we met Margaret. We've had a wonderful life, haven't we?"

Oliver chuckled. "I remember those parties well. I once told Bertrand how disappointed I was that he'd managed to sweep you off your feet before I had a chance."

Her cheeks warmed at his words. "And I remember Bertrand telling you that you were far too young for me," she replied with a laugh. "Even though we were the same age."

"Well, I had some growing up to do, and you were definitely off the market," Oliver said. "But I'm not too young anymore, am I?"

Ginger's heart quickened as she met his gaze. There was something there, an unexpected spark of interest she couldn't deny. "I like to think we're still young at heart."

Oliver touched her hand, and she responded, twining her fingers with his. Oliver held her gaze. "I'd love to visit Summer Beach soon. Would it be alright if I called on you?"

For a moment, Ginger was transported back in time, feeling like the young woman who had first arrived in Los Angeles, full of dreams and possibilities. But she wasn't that woman anymore. She was a grandmother and great-grandmother, a woman with a lifetime of experiences behind her.

And yet, she was still a woman.

"I'd like that, Oliver. We have so much history and so many stories to share. I'll introduce you to my family."

"I would like that very much," he said, his voice dropping a notch.

Oliver and Margaret had never had children, and she

sensed an air of loneliness about him. She raised her glass. "Here's to seeing you in Summer Beach."

As they clinked glasses, the last rays of sunlight glinted off the crystal, and a flutter of excitement filled Ginger. Maybe life still had surprises in store for her.

## 13

*W*ith Scout trotting beside him, Jack strolled along the wooden deck of the marina, which was quiet at this time of day. He'd chosen this spot to talk to Blake because of that.

Jack had spent the morning with a contractor and a crew to repair the rear deck. He couldn't leave Scout outside with them in case he slipped out, and the dog couldn't be trusted inside on his own. Not after he'd opened the closet door and chewed Marina's best sneakers to shreds.

Many of the boats were nestled in their slips today. The mayor's vintage craft was at the end, and Tyler's sleek boat bobbed near the front. Mitch, who owned Java Beach, looked like he was preparing his boat for one of his afternoon shoreline cruise charters. Jack waved at him.

He walked back and waited near the front, rocking on his heels. The ocean breeze ruffled his hair as he watched Blake approach. The younger man was dressed like a regular guy in a nice pair of jeans and a collared knit shirt with his organization's logo.

What Jack knew of him, he liked. Blake seemed intelligent and straightforward. He was well-educated and passionate about ocean rescue. For Heather's sake, Jack hoped he wasn't wrong about him.

He'd find out today.

Blake greeted him with a confident, friendly handshake and reached down to pet Scout. "It's good to see you, but what's so urgent? Is it Heather?"

"She's fine for now. But we need to talk. Marina and I met your parents."

Blake shook his head. "They're a pair, for sure." His brow furrowed as he noticed Jack's serious expression. "Wait, what happened?"

"You haven't heard from your parents?"

"No. What's going on?"

Blake looked like he had no idea what had transpired. "Let's take a walk," Jack replied. The sturdy wooden deck creaked under their weight as they set off.

Jack hated interrogating Heather's fiancé, but the news was better coming from him than Marina or Heather. "Your father told us you're engaged to another woman. Care to explain that?"

Blake's face paled. "Oh, no. Did Marina tell Heather?"

"Not yet," Jack replied. "I wanted to give you a chance to sort this out with your parents and Heather. But I'm not sure how long Marina can keep from saying something to her. She's awfully upset." He fixed Blake with a steady gaze. "What do you have to say for yourself? Is it true?"

Blake ran a hand through his hair, his frustration

evident. "It's complicated. My father's partner had a daughter, and we grew up together. Priscilla and I dated for a couple of months in high school, and it was sort of serious, but we went our separate ways for college. That was the end of it. However, our parents made assumptions, and Priscilla never corrected them."

"And you didn't think to mention this to Heather?" Jack asked, disappointed in his story.

Blake shook his head. "It's been years now. I thought Priscilla would find someone and get married. I didn't think it was important."

"Well, it is now."

"Yeah, I know. I guess Priscilla is still interested, but I'm not. That's why I avoid events where I know she'll be. Our folks still throw us together."

Jack sighed. "So why are your parents—especially your father—so set on Priscilla for you?"

"Yeah. That's where it gets complicated. It's all about money and business."

Blake's tone had a bitter edge Jack hadn't heard before. No, not bitterness. Frustration. "Explain it to me. You're going to have to tell Heather everything."

"I see that now." Blake drew a hand across his face. "Dad's been working on his estate and retirement plan. There's a lot of money at stake, along with tax implications. If something happens to either partner, they don't want an outsider coming in and taking over. Essentially, everything would be easier if Priscilla and I were married. We would inherit equally, and the business would go on." He shook his head. "Her father isn't well, so Dad is getting nervous."

"That's a lot to consider. I imagine it's hard to turn your back on that."

Blake met Jack's gaze with fierce determination. "I don't care about the business or the money. I love what I do, and it pays enough for me to be comfortable and have a family. I don't need to throw money around on fancy cars and airplanes like my father does. I grew up with that. Why do you think I became an aquatic veterinarian?"

"Animals are nicer than people, huh?"

"Many of them. Not Heather, or you guys, though. She's the best thing that's ever happened to me."

"Hey, I know how that feels." Jack nodded, processing this information. "For the record, your mother apologized. She seemed embarrassed by the whole situation."

"She is," Blake admitted. "She knows Priscilla isn't right for me, but she has to live with my dad. Their marriage has been rocky for years. It's a primer on what not to do in a relationship." Blake scrubbed his face in irritation.

A heavy silence fell between them, broken by waves lapping the boats. Scout panted patiently beside them.

Finally, Blake asked, "So, will you tell Heather?"

Jack shook his head firmly. "That's your job, my man. But you'd better do it fast and let her hear from you. This isn't the kind of secret that stays buried for long."

"I'm seeing her tonight." Blake's shoulders slumped with the weight of the task ahead.

If the younger man's words were true, Jack was truly sorry for him. He'd hear about it soon enough.

Watching Blake's retreating figure, Jack made a mental note to check in with Marina. They would have a difficult conversation ahead, deciding how to tell Heather if Blake didn't come clean soon. Jack couldn't shake the feeling that this was just the beginning of a complicated situation.

"Come on, Scout," Jack said. "We have another stop."

After leaving Blake, Jack drove to Ginger's house for an afternoon working session. He opened the van, and Scout rocketed toward the garden. He let out a sharp whistle, catching the dog's attention. "Don't you dare, buddy."

Ginger swung the door open with a bright smile. "Good afternoon, Jack. May we stop by the Hidden Garden first? Leilani and Roy have some items ready for me to pick up, and I'd like to speak to them about an idea. Do you have enough space in that van for a few items?"

"Absolutely, happy to help," Jack replied, giving her a warm smile as he helped her into the van.

Scout gave him a puzzled look but hopped back in with enthusiasm.

After driving the short distance and parking in front of the nursery, Jack opened the door for Ginger. Scout hopped out, and Jack snapped a leash on the dog's collar.

Once past the entryway filled with fountains and flowers, they saw Leilani and Roy Miyake, the proprietors.

A squirrel darted ahead, and Jack pulled on the lead to restrain Scout.

"Leilani, dear," Ginger said, taking the other woman's hands. "Thank you for arranging my order for me. I'd also like to discuss reserving your lovely nursery for a special party. I spoke to Heather this morning, and she likes the idea."

Jack's gut churned at that. Depending on Heather's reaction, that engagement might be short-lived.

"Excuse me," he said to Ginger. "Would you like to have a look around first?"

"In a moment," Ginger replied, waving him off.

Leilani said, "We've had parties here before. We string fairy lights in the trees, and the garden looks magical."

Ginger nodded. "I attended one here. Now, about Heather and Blake."

Concerned, Jack tried again. "Ginger, if I might have a word first." He had to buy time for Blake to talk to Heather.

Ginger ignored him, so he was left with little choice. He dropped Scout's lead.

The Labrador retriever streaked after the squirrel, scattering potted plants as he careened through the outdoor nursery with his slightly off-kilter gait.

Leilani waved her arms at her husband. "Roy, would you stop him?"

"Slow down, old boy," her husband called back, gripping Scout's collar.

"I'm sorry," Jack said to Ginger. "Scout is easily excited. I'll load your purchases, and we can return another day."

To Leilani, he added, "I'm happy to pay for the damage here."

"It's not the first time," Leilani said, shrugging off his offer. "Plenty of people bring dogs. Plants grow back."

"You should control that dog in public places." Looking a little annoyed, Ginger sighed. "Perhaps this wasn't fair of me. I know we have work to do."

"Roy is happy to deliver whatever you need," Leilani said.

She smiled at that. "I'll call you tomorrow, and we'll check the dates."

After loading the van with Ginger's purchases—supplies for the sprinkler system, plant food, a new rake, and a selection of indoor plants—Jack returned with her to her cottage.

On her private patio, Ginger relaxed under a coral canvas umbrella. Scout stretched out on the stone pavers beside her while Jack opened his notebook, ready to hear more of her story.

"I'd like to hear about when you lived in Washington, D.C. I understand you met scores of interesting people there."

As Ginger sipped her tea, her gaze rested on the outdoor fireplace decorated with colorful Mexican Talavera tiles, and her memories began to flow.

"After Bertrand was recalled to the States, we settled in Virginia with a townhouse in Washington. Near Embassy Row in Georgetown, to be exact. As quiet and orderly as my work was during the day, Bertrand's career was often the opposite. We attended several functions every week, and he often had dinner meetings, leaving me at home with Sandi, though I never minded."

Jack sensed a certain reticence now. His journalistic instincts were on high alert, and he suspected she was holding something back.

"Your life will read more like a novel than a biography," he said, trying to loosen her thoughts. "The people you've known, the circles you've moved in. It's extraordinary."

"A novel, indeed." She smiled at the idea. "You flatter

me, Jack. But a life well lived should be a page-turner, don't you think?"

"I'll do my best."

While he waited for her to continue, he glanced at Scout, still lounging contentedly beside the table. The dog's ears perked before he relaxed again.

Jack tapped record on his phone. "During that time, you and Bertrand met some of the most influential people of the 20th century. Care to drop a few names?"

Ginger's eyes gleamed at his question. "In Washington, D.C., we met with several presidents. In France, Bertrand knew President de Gaulle. And later, we met Prime Minister Margaret Thatcher at numerous events on both sides of the Atlantic—she was quite accomplished."

She continued, recalling encounters and friendships forged with other heads of state, politicians, and celebrities. "Everyone adored Bertrand and gravitated toward him. He was a natural leader and communicator."

"I would say the same about you." Jack considered how he might weave these vignettes into a narrative as he listened. Ginger's life was a tapestry of personal triumphs against world-changing events.

How could he capture the essence of this remarkable woman without losing the intimacy of her journey or the gravity of her professional accomplishments?

Jack tapped his pen thoughtfully against his notepad. "In your work, you've mentioned developing a deeper motivation. Can you tell me more about that?"

Ginger's eyes looked distant, as if she were gazing into the past. "My work was often critical to world affairs—at home and abroad. What mattered to me was making a difference in a rapidly changing world. The Cold War was at its height, and I felt a strong responsibility. Not just to my country, but to the shared future we were all trying to shape."

Jack leaned forward, intrigued. "So it wasn't only about the intellectual challenge?"

"That was certainly part of it," Ginger replied. "But there was an urgency, a sense that what we were doing could tip the scales of history. Every pattern uncovered and every code we broke fed into the larger picture of diplomatic relations. We were on the front lines of a silent war fought with information. Correspondence sometimes revealed other serious issues."

She expanded on that, mentioning a high-profile trial for espionage. Jack was surprised; he hadn't known of her involvement behind the scenes.

"And how did Bertrand factor into all this?" Jack asked, scribbling notes even while the digital time on the recorder flashed.

Ginger's face softened. "Bertrand was my anchor through the storm. Our townhouse in Washington became a hub of activity—cocktail parties for visitors, diplomatic soirees, meetings disguised as dinner parties."

"Sounds like something out of a spy novel."

"Art has imitated life since Plato's time," Ginger said. Almost as an afterthought, she added, "Sometimes, it's the other way around, for better or worse."

Jack noticed a touch of regret in her voice and made a note. "It sounds like an intense time."

"It was," Ginger agreed. "But it was also exhilarating.

We were part of something bigger than ourselves. And yet..."

"And yet?" Jack asked, prompting her.

Ginger turned back with a guarded expression. "Life has a way of dishing up the unexpected." She glanced at her watch. "That's a story for another time."

Jack nodded, recognizing the subtle shift in Ginger's demeanor. He knew better than to push too hard. Instead, he jotted down a few more notes, weighing options for structuring this complex narrative.

Ginger reached across the table, patting his hand affectionately. "Thank you for listening. I trust you to tell this story."

They sat in companionable silence, sipping the last of their tea. Jack was determined to do justice to Ginger's life story. Still, between her recollections and his research, he had a nagging feeling that the two might not mesh.

It wasn't what she said, but what she held back. Somewhere was the truth, and he would find it. After all, that's what he did.

## 14

*A*fter finishing her presentation on basic computer skills for the senior center in Summer Beach, Ginger closed her laptop computer and set it aside on the red Formica kitchen table where she'd worked for years, watching soup simmering on the stove or bread baking in the oven.

She had taught classes at the senior center for a long time, and now many attendees were younger than she was. But then, they hadn't had her experience.

Stairs creaked and footsteps shuffled across the living room floor. When Heather appeared in the doorway still wearing her beach-themed pajamas, Ginger looked up.

Instantly, she could see something was troubling her. "You're up early. Ready for coffee?"

"Please." Heather plunked herself in a chair and leaned her head on the table. Her tangled, dark blond hair spilled over her arms.

Ginger poured a cup and placed it in front of her,

waiting for her to share her problems, as she often did. Heather and Marina were close, too. Still, Ginger enjoyed listening and offering advice when she could. That was part of the joy of being the matriarch of the family, a role she relished, although it hadn't always been easy.

After her graduation in a few months, Heather would marry and leave. Once again, the cottage would be quiet. At least having the cafe nearby gave Ginger a social outlet.

She joined Heather and opened her laptop, adding to her document until Heather was ready to talk. With so much business online, from banking to managing health-care, seniors needed guidance accessing websites and making safe transactions.

She also emphasized caution because there were many scams. She advised people not to click through unexpected emails from banks but to go directly to the site. And not to give out sensitive details over the phone—they should call the company directly. She paused, thinking of other tips she could add.

After Heather had a few sips of coffee, she heaved a long sigh. "Got a minute to talk?"

Ginger closed her computer. "What's on your mind, dear?"

Heather rubbed her hands over her reddened eyes. "Blake and I had a long talk last night, and I don't know what to do. Mom and Jack drove to Orange County to meet his parents at some out-of-the-way cafe Blake said they never go to. Like they were embarrassed to meet them."

Her voice caught. "And then, his dad started talking—didn't even let them order anything to eat, even though they had invited them for dinner—and made some outrageous claim about Blake already being engaged to someone else."

Ginger was shocked and sorry to hear this. "That sounds quite rude, but Blake isn't responsible for his parents' boorish behavior." Marina hadn't mentioned this yet, but they'd both been busy.

"He said it's mainly his father. His mom supposedly apologized. They don't get along very well."

"And you still haven't met them?"

Heather shook her head. "Blake says they're always busy, but now I'm wondering if this is why he didn't want me to."

"Sadly, not every family is close." Ginger lifted a lock of Heather's hair before it dipped into her coffee. "What did Blake have to say about this claim they made?"

"He totally denies it. He said he dated her in high school, but that's long over. Ten years ago. But she still likes him, and their parents have promised them huge inheritances if they get married. Something about taxes and partnership agreements that I don't understand. Priscilla is her name. She's all for it, but he's not."

"Sounds like an arranged marriage." Ginger didn't think Blake was the type to agree to that. "Do you think the inheritance is important to him, or might be someday?"

Heather chewed her lip for a moment. "Blake says he doesn't want any part of that scheme. He can support himself just fine. His father has threatened to disinherit him if we marry, but Blake doesn't care."

Ginger nodded, piecing together the story. "It sounds like he has thought it through."

"I can't imagine someone turning down a huge windfall, though." Heather sniffed. "Blake says that when you grow up like that, it's just stuff. He wants to be happy."

"I can understand that. He certainly seems to be with you."

With a frown, Heather asked, "But what if he regrets that decision someday?"

"None of us can project into the future, and nothing is assured." Ginger fell silent for a moment, recalling when her world fell apart. "In life, we must trust each other and take chances. If you truly love each other and keep the lines of communication open, you have an excellent chance. Blake didn't choose his parents."

A tentative smile bloomed on Heather's reddened face. "I want to believe him."

"Has he shown you any reasons why you shouldn't?"

"Only this incident with his parents."

"Which is out of his control. Don't let them destroy your relationship as they have destroyed their own. Some people feel unworthy of happiness, so they inflict that on everyone around them, too. Keep your distance, and don't let them."

"Sounds easy, but I don't think it will be."

Ginger stood and wrapped her arms around Heather's shoulders. "You'd be surprised what a strong statement the single word *no* is."

Heather almost laughed at that.

"Say yes to your young man." Ginger kissed her on the cheek.

Smiling now, Heather said, "I'll call him before he leaves for work and tell him I'm okay." She refilled her coffee and turned around. "Oh, hey, did you see the letter I left in the study for you? It came when you were out with Jack yesterday. It looked personal. I'll get it for you."

Heather returned shortly with the letter.

"Thank you, dear." Ginger glanced at the return address and smiled, pocketing it. She would open it later.

For now, she had work to do. Feeling a sense of relief for Heather, Ginger returned to the kitchen and opened her computer to finish her presentation. She planned to meet with Jack again today. Maybe she would tell him about her early work with computers. She hadn't thought of Commodore Hopper in years. Rear Admiral, that is. Lower half.

As she shifted in her chair, Oliver's letter crinkled its presence in her pocket. She would read it when she had time to relax and savor it.

---

LISTENING to the latest Elvis Presley song playing in the background to drown the noise of the computers, Ginger's fingers flew across the keyboard, her eyes fixed on the glowing green text on the computer screen. The whir of the giant machine fans filled the air, punctuated by the rhythmic clacking of keys.

She pulled her sweater around her shoulders and shivered. The room was kept cold to cool the massive computers that took up half the floor space.

She had been selected for this assignment and was eager to use her mathematical skills in an emerging field. Computing was evolving at a breakneck pace and would change the world—and her work—as she'd known it.

Ginger was assigned to the COBOL programming language project. She found it exciting because it was the first computer language created with common language commands, so it could be used by a wider variety of people, such as those in business. *If x, then y, else z.* She was helping to further this word-based language.

"How are you doing, Ginger?"

Ginger looked up to see her mentor, Grace Hopper, looking at her with curiosity and admiration.

"I've just tested this code, and it's working now," Ginger replied.

Grace nodded approvingly. "Excellent work. Your contributions to the COBOL project have been invaluable. Have you considered my offer to stay on with the team?"

"My husband will be returning from overseas soon, so I won't be able to. But I've enjoyed contributing."

While Bertrand was away these past months, she had rented a furnished duplex for herself, Sandi, and an *au pair*, who was happy to travel with Ginger and see more of the United States. In this case, Pennsylvania. But Bertrand was hinting at a possible relocation for them and had asked her to meet him at their townhouse when he arrived home.

"You're welcome to return anytime," Grace said. "You have keen insights to problems that require sophisticated solutions. Perhaps you could work on a consulting basis for special assignments?"

"I'd like that," Ginger replied. "There are times I could be available." She had also worked on projects at universities in Boston. This kept Ginger mentally occupied. Sandi was too young to be in school, and Bertrand was gaining experience across several European countries, so she was taking advantage of opportunities.

"Let's coordinate on those times," Grace said. "Your help in advancing this project is greatly needed. You share my vision that computers can be used more widely."

"Thank you," Ginger said, humbled at her mentor's trust.

Ginger thought COBOL was revolutionary and could see how it would spread the use of computers beyond the office of mathematicians and scientists who had to laboriously code each command.

She recalled the secretarial work she had performed for Kurt. She thought executives and secretaries could be trained to use programming languages for repetitive tasks like payroll.

A decade ago, Grace Hopper developed the pioneering A-0 compiler, a groundbreaking tool that transformed complex mathematical code into machine-readable instructions. That innovation marked a significant leap forward. Next, Grace suggested a revolutionary idea: writing programs using words instead of symbols. Despite being told it would never work, she persisted. Her team successfully developed FLOW-MATIC, the first programming language to use word commands.

COBOL was derived from that, and Ginger was helping to refine it.

Grace's eyes lit with another thought. "Would you consider writing a paper on your work for publication?"

Ginger shook her head. "I don't have the educational credentials, but I could contribute or write the article under someone else's name on the team."

Grace nodded. "You're likely correct. That is a prudent decision, if unfortunate."

"Knowing my work has value is enough for me," Ginger added. She didn't need to call attention to herself.

She had security clearance now and seldom discussed her work with anyone outside her immediate team. She'd settled on the term statistician to describe her work. Few knew what that entailed, so she was generally safe at cocktail parties. For those who did, she could discuss recent studies or theories before turning the conversation to the latest Broadway play.

Life with Bertrand was always exciting. As much as she loved her work, if they moved overseas again, she would welcome that experience, too. She loved living in Paris, and they could easily travel to other countries by train.

Sometimes, she could hardly believe this was her life. When she wrote to her mother in the evenings, she described her new experiences, which delighted her mother. And when they visited Summer Beach, Ginger enjoyed spending time there.

While their lovely cottage there was home, she and Bertrand weren't ready to leave their professional lives.

# 15

hile Bertrand cracked crab for lunch on the beach, Ginger sat on the sun-drenched porch of her cottage, carefully watching her grandchildren play in the sand far from the water.

Marina, the eldest at eight, was busy constructing an elaborate sandcastle, filling and emptying a bright red bucket. Six-year-old Brooke chased seagulls; her delighted squeals carried on the ocean breeze. At just a year old, little Kai was tucked safely in Ginger's arms, watching her sisters and waving her tiny hands, eager to be a part of their fun.

The front screen door creaked open. Bertrand's voice broke through her reverie as he handed her a glass of iced tea. "Thought you could use a refresher, darling."

Taking the cool glass, Ginger smiled up at him. She thought her husband was still the most handsome man in any room. He remained fit, and the gray strands sprinkled across his thick hair made him look more distinguished.

She sipped the iced tea. "I've been thinking about how easy and peaceful life is here on this sunny beach."

Bertrand eased onto the swing beside her. "Someday, we'll make it our full-time home. I have another five, maybe ten years to work. But you may return as often as you wish to see our grandchildren."

"With my parents gone, it seems different now." She sighed at her memories, now tucked away in photo albums. "We have become the older generation."

Bertrand laughed at that. "We're forever young in our hearts and minds. Just not the knees."

"Swimming is good for that," Ginger replied, although she missed him on the morning hikes they used to take. Still, he was ten years older, so she had to be considerate.

"Nothing beats the pool at the Ritz, unless it's Biarritz," he said, his eyes twinkling. "How about we make reservations at the Hôtel du Palais when we return? You love the coastline."

She considered that for a moment. "That's a wonderful idea. The food and views are spectacular." Several years ago, they had returned to Paris, which they both loved. Bertrand had earned his seniority and was well respected.

Still, they returned to Summer Beach when they could. She gestured toward the beach and their grandchildren. "However, this area has a unique draw."

Bertrand put his arm around his wife and pinched little Kai's cheek. "I promise we'll come back more often. And one day, we might never want to leave."

Just then, Sandi arrived at the house in her car. She pushed her sunglasses up over her wavy strawberry-blond hair. She looked slightly frazzled but happy. "Mom, Dad, thanks for watching the kids. I hope they weren't too much trouble. Dennis is finishing his meeting, but I thought I'd come back early."

Ginger waved off her daughter's concerns. "The children were a delight. Although I must say, keeping up with them can be more challenging than work."

Bertrand laughed. "Fortunately, you're practiced in problem-solving."

As Sandi lifted her baby, Ginger felt a sense of contentment wash over her. She had accomplished so much in her career, contributed to advancements that would shape the future of technology and security. But here, at this moment, she realized that her greatest legacy might be the love and knowledge she could pass on to these bright-eyed children.

"I'm ready when you are," she said to Bertrand.

"Speaking of being ready, fresh crab and corn on the cob awaits in the kitchen," he said, rising. "Who is hungry?"

Sandi stashed her sunglasses in her bag. "If you have enough, Dennis and I will stay."

"That's why I steamed as much as I did." Bertrand flexed an arm. "Real men don't cook small portions."

Sandi laughed. "Gee, Dad, I didn't expect such a caveman comment from you."

"I keep up with the times, my darling daughter. Will you help me in the kitchen?"

"I'll gather the girls," Ginger said. "They're a mess, so let's eat on the rear patio."

"You can hose them off there," Sandi said.

"Just like I used to do for you when we visited," Ginger said, remembering those summers with fondness.

Ginger called the girls from the beach, and they followed her around the side of the cottage to the patio. Marina and Brooke giggled with delight as she sprayed off the sand with a hose. She dried them with thick beach towels until they were relatively clean.

Sandi's voice floated through the screen door to Ginger.

"We've just landed our first accounting clients, Dad, so we gave our notice at work."

"I'm sure you and Dennis will do well," Bertrand replied.

"He wants to prove himself to you and Mom."

"We've always thought well of him."

"I know," Sandi said. "He's still sensitive about his background. Having been in foster care, he's never felt like he fit in."

"Growing up overseas isn't as glamorous as most people think," Bertrand said. "You struggled to fit in, too."

"Now I look at going to school overseas as an adventure that few others had." Sandi glanced outside to check on her children. "We found office space, so we'll open the new business soon."

"What sort of clients are you looking for?"

"The ones Dennis brought in are investors. They own casinos and racetracks in Nevada, California, and other states. Dennis is brilliant with those sort of complicated tax returns."

Bertrand was quiet for a moment. "Those are tough businesses, and the people running them can be difficult. Promise me you'll be careful around those types?"

"Oh, Dad. Dennis knows what he's doing. We'll make a fortune from their work alone."

Although Dennis was bright, charming, and held master's degrees in accounting, Ginger wondered if their son-in-law knew what he was doing.

# 16

*M*arina brought the deep tart pan with its buttery crust from the oven to let it rest. She glanced at Jack, who was diligently tearing lettuce for a salad at the new kitchen island they'd added.

He looked far too serious.

She whirled around and stole a kiss. "Thanks for preparing that, sweetheart."

Jack broke into a smile. "Why not? I like to eat, too. And that Leo can sure put the food away these days."

"How's Ginger's story coming along?" Marina asked, stirring the tomato basil soup.

"Honestly, it's incredible," Jack replied, his voice filled with wonder. "Her life reads like a novel. The way she followed her heart, blazing trails for women in math and science, blending her professional and family life. It's inspiring today, but back when women had fewer options, that took nerve. She blithely forged on, being the best version of herself she could be." He chuckled. "That probably infuriated some people."

Marina laughed. "She once said that you don't have to know your place. Your place is wherever you decide it is."

"Ginger was not easily dissuaded, that's for sure." Jack quartered a small tomato as he talked.

"She never took no for an answer," Marina added. "She simply figured out how to do whatever she wanted."

"You're a lot like her." Jack paused to select a cucumber. "However, I've noticed she doesn't care about taking credit for her achievements."

"That's always been true. She's too busy moving on to the next challenge. But she loved being the Grand Marshall in the parade."

"That she did. I wonder if there has ever been anything she couldn't handle."

"Such as what?" Marina asked, pouring smoked bacon into the cooled crust.

"A disappointment or tragedy. Many people hit bottom —even the Gingers of the world."

Marina's journalistic instincts kicked in. *Was Jack fishing for material?* She hesitated, then relaxed. He was family now, and this book was about Ginger, after all.

"She took our parents' deaths awfully hard," Marina said. "We all did, of course. She had to be strong for us, but I could always tell."

"I know that was devastating for all of you," Jack said, sweeping her into his arms. "And for her, losing her only child."

Marina nodded. "She was especially distraught over my mom—it was like they'd left something unfinished. Just a feeling I always had." She lifted a shoulder and let it fall. "But I suppose that's common. I never got to tell Stan we were pregnant."

"That's an interesting observation," Jack said slowly. "And I'm sorry you had to go through that." He kissed her on the cheek and released her.

Marina took out eggs and heavy cream from the refrigerator. "Anyway, all the amazing people she and Grandpa knew should add to her story. When do you think you'll have a first draft completed?"

"I still have some research to do. So, after the holidays, I imagine. I'll edit it in the spring. I don't want to pitch it until it's finished."

Just then, Leo burst through the back door. "Is dinner ready yet?"

Jack mussed his son's hair. "We'll have soup and salad first."

Marina added a pinch of nutmeg before pouring the egg and cream mixture into the tart pan. She opened the hot oven and eased her creation onto a rack. Another commotion sounded at the front door.

"Hey, Mom." Heather's excited voice filled the house. "I'm here with Blake."

Marina and Jack exchanged quick glances when the pair appeared in the kitchen doorway.

Blake spoke quickly. "First, I want to apologize for my parents' behavior. I assure you, none of what they said was true." He hugged Heather close to his side. "I love your daughter very much, and we've done a lot of talking."

"Everything is okay, Mom." Heather held out her arms, and Marina embraced her.

"I'm so relieved for you," Marina said, smiling. "And thank you for letting us know, Blake."

Jack gave Blake a bro hug. "You did good, man."

Blake grinned at that. "My mom called again this afternoon. She told me that night with you guys was the final humiliation, as she put it. She just kicked out my father, and this time, I think she means it."

"I'm so sorry to hear that," Marina said, feeling a little guilty, although that man had it coming.

"Don't be," Blake replied. "She sounds better already. Dad is a bully, and he has lessons to learn. At the very least, they need a long break from each other. And she wants to get to know Heather."

Marina shot her daughter a guarded look.

"It's okay, Mom. Blake says she's fine without his dad around."

Marina recalled her whirlwind of emotions at that age. "We're here to help in any way we can. Are you hungry? We have tomato basil soup, Jack's salad, sweet potato fries, and a quiche Lorraine in about half an hour."

"Oh my gosh, that's my favorite comfort dish," Heather said, her eyes widening. "With a side salad and sweet potato fries with garlic aioli. That must go in your cookbook."

"Now I know," Blake said, kissing her cheek. He and Heather set the table on the deck so they could all eat outdoors.

"I've already included it," Marina said. She'd started compiling some recipes.

Scout plopped nearby, likely waiting for table treats. "No beggars by the table, please." Marina nudged him to one side.

As Heather carried dishes to the table, she said, "I can hardly wait to start working on the food truck and marketing part of the business after graduation. I have so many ideas."

Marina recognized the spark of determination in her daughter's eyes—the same spark she'd seen so often in Ginger's. And her sisters. They all had that. "There will be time enough for all that. You have courses to finish and a wedding to plan."

"Aunt Kai said she wants to help with everything."

"Go easy on her. She's enthusiastic, but she tires easily right now." Marina turned back to the stove, furrowing her brow as she thought of Kai. The excitement of Heather's engagement had distracted her.

"Is Aunt Kai okay, Mom?" Heather asked, looking concerned.

"Brooke went with her to the doctor, and everything seemed normal, but I'm still concerned," Marina admitted. "She's had more than the usual pregnancy symptoms. The doctor agreed to run more tests."

Jack came up behind her, placing a comforting hand on her shoulder. "Kai's strong, and she has a good medical team."

Marina nodded, leaning into his touch. "I know, but she's my sister, so I'm still concerned."

"What can I do?" Heather asked.

"Call her occasionally. Kai would like that." Marina added, "I'll keep you all updated."

Leo, who had been quietly listening, spoke up. "Let's make Aunt Kai a care package with her favorite snacks, some girly socks, and candles. That made my mom happy when she was sick."

A rush of love for her sweet stepson swept through Marina, and she leaned in for a hug. "That's a wonderful idea, and I'm sure she'd appreciate it. Let's do that tomorrow. And I'm so glad your mother feels great now."

After dinner, Heather and Blake insisted on cleaning up while Leo took a shower before bedtime.

Sitting outside, Marina leaned into Jack's arms. These were the quiet moments of the day she cherished with him. Still, something in his expression earlier when he asked about Ginger had concerned her. She hoped he would be as respectful as he always was with her, even if he didn't get the answers he wanted.

# 17

*A*n idea struck Ginger, and she looked up from her work of meticulously converting recipe measurements. "How about this as a title, *The Sunny Coast Table: Recipes from the Coral Café?*"

"I love it," Marina said, her eyes brightening. "We've been through a hundred titles."

Heather pumped her fist in the air. "At least. I like it, too. How about you, Aunt Kai?"

"That brings to mind a good visual; I can work with that." Absently Kai smoothed a hand over her rounded belly.

Ginger stretched her arms above her head, surveying the chaos spread across her expansive dining table. Stacks of recipe cards, handwritten notes, printed text, and photographs covered the surface.

This cookbook was a welcome diversion from the work on her biography with Jack. He could be intense, but she knew that was only due to his adherence to professional excellence.

"I can't believe how much we've accomplished with everyone's input," Marina said, a note of pride in her voice.

Ginger smiled at their small team. "It's coming together beautifully. I knew we could do it. You'll have a book ready for the spring crowd." Meeting that date was necessary, they'd decided.

Heather, hunched over a notepad, her pen flying across the page, chimed in without looking up. "Mom, remember when we thought the shrimp and pesto pizza was just a wild experiment? Now it's practically our signature dish."

Marina laughed, reaching for a photo of her bestselling pizza.

Ginger was pleased with the overall organization she and Marina had decided on. They had easily populated most sections. "Where would you like to put the quiche Lorraine?"

"It could be served any time of day." Marina shuffled through printouts. "Be sure we include the quiche variations, especially Ethan's favorite with Gruyère cheese. We're light on breakfast recipes. Or we could add a section called Anytime Favorites."

The afternoon sun streamed through the windows as they worked, although the air was growing slightly crisp. Ginger pulled a lightweight sweater over her cotton blouse. Fortunately, Summer Beach temperatures were mild year-round. Winter was when their grapefruit and lemons began to ripen.

"We should get some beautiful photos of the orchard to include in the book," she suggested.

Kai looked up. "I can do that. I might have some from last year, too."

"The food photos you took the other day are fantastic," Marina said.

Ginger eyed her youngest granddaughter, wary of her condition. Brooke was likely to deliver her fourth child early, but Ginger was especially concerned about her sister. "How are you feeling these days, Kai?"

"Much better, but I wish this little one would hurry up and get here."

Kai was energetic, but Ginger knew getting enough rest was important, especially in the last trimester. "You should pace yourself with the holiday performance."

"Axe is mostly managing that," Kai replied, waving off her concern. "Construction work slows during the winter holidays."

"I appreciate your taking the time to help," Marina said, touching her sister's hand.

"You've done most of it," Kai said. "Who knew you'd be such a whiz at dictation?"

Looking up from the manuscript, Ginger added, "Your writing is wonderful, dear. You have a real talent for bringing the recipes to life. And your photos are lovely, Kai." She held one up. "I can see this one of Marina at the family table on the cover."

To Ginger, this cookbook was more than just a collection of recipes; it was a testament to their family's creativity and resilience. She was happy to support Marina in this effort.

"Oh, look at this one," Heather exclaimed, holding up a

photo of a cupcake tower. "Remember when we made these for the birthday party?"

Marina smiled. "We were frosting them right up until the last minute. I'll add those recipes, too."

Ginger enjoyed listening to the happy chatter while they continued to sort through photos and make notes on recipes, punctuated by bursts of laughter as they remembered good times and delicious dishes.

Over the course of the afternoon, the scene around the table was soon transformed. The chaos of scattered papers and photos gave way to neat stacks of organized documents. Ginger was pleased with their accomplishment.

With her laptop open, Marina stared at the screen with satisfaction. "We've come so far. Most of the recipes are written up now."

"Brooke has offered to manage a team of local recipe testers," Ginger said. "She's gathered neighbors and other gardeners to help. Maybe we can add some locals from the farmers market. I can reach out to Cookie."

"That would be great," Marina said. "Thank you for all you're doing."

Heather lowered a piece of paper. "The introduction sounds great, Ginger. I love the history of the Coral Cottage before the cafe. And how your friend Julia inspired some of the recipes."

"It's all true," Ginger said. "Although we've edited them over the years, adding and subtracting ingredients, especially using our local produce." She tapped a notepad filled with calculations. "The conversion from restaurant-sized portions to home kitchen amounts is complete, as is the imperial-to-metric measurements conversion."

Marina nodded, looking pleased. "I couldn't have done that without your precision. With all of us testing in our kitchens, we can confirm measurements."

"Everything is coming together," Ginger said, ticking off a list she was keeping. "Your method of dictating recipes while you cooked brought the descriptions to life."

Heather brightened. "Now that you've got the system down, Mom, you should keep going. A food truck cookbook would really sell. People love comfort food. And I have a great title."

"So do I," Kai said, laughing. "*Food Truck and Theater Bites*. We'll sell it at the Seashell. Remember, that was the original venue for the food truck."

"We'll work on that," Marina said, smiling.

Ginger was so proud of them. This project was a team effort, with each of them contributing.

"I have a meeting with a graphic designer next week," Marina continued. "She's excited to work on the layout with Kai's photos."

"I'm sure it will be beautiful." Ginger could picture the finished product in her mind. "I can already imagine it on sale at the cafe and in kitchens everywhere. This book will likely beat Jack's to print."

"Your biography is more involved," Marina said, frowning slightly. "Jack is conducting a great deal of research and wants to get the tone just right for you. How is it going with him?"

"He should be finished with my recollections," Ginger said. "One can only talk about themselves for so long."

Still, Ginger wanted to leave this legacy for her family and other young women interested in science, math, and technology. She trusted Jack to make it sound exciting, even if he had excavated a few unpleasant memories. She preferred to focus on the positive aspects of her life.

"I know it's premature," Heather began, "but I've been thinking about marketing strategies for the book debut. I can use this for my last semester's capstone project. It should be a real-life application."

Ginger nodded, impressed by her initiative. She was pleased Heather would stay on at the cafe and knew Marina was, too.

"What did you have in mind?" Marina asked.

Heather checked her notes. "I propose we use the cafe as our primary launch pad. We could set up a display, plan a book signing launch party, and offer a special cookbook menu featuring recipes from the book. You could do cooking demonstrations at the farmers market with those recipes and offer those items and the cookbook for sale. That's just for starters."

"I like the menu idea," Marina said, making a note.

Ginger smiled, reminded of her culinary adventures with her friend in Cambridge. "That sounds wonderful. It's amazing how far we've come from our early days in the kitchen."

Heather continued with her excitement building. "I've created a list of local and regional media outlets. We could invite food critics to the cafe for a tasting event and give them an early preview of the cookbook."

Marina nodded approvingly but cautioned her. "All good ideas, but we need to be careful about managing our time. You have one last semester and a wedding to plan."

"A beach wedding won't be too hard," Heather said,

smiling. "I want it sort of like yours and Jack's, Mom."

Heather went on. "As for other marketing, I can focus on social media. It's cost-effective and has a wide reach. We'll use those videos Aunt Kai took of us cooking to create short, engaging content."

"Be careful not to overextend yourself," Marina said to her daughter. "With the second truck up and running now, I need to standardize menus and operations before going further."

Ginger knew this was a particular passion of Heather's.

"I've been researching franchise models for my class," Heather said, citing some franchise cost ranges and statistics. "If we standardize the recipes for the cookbook, that can be the first step toward franchising the food trucks regionally."

"She's a smart one," Ginger said with a nod of approval.

Kai made a face. "I'm glad you think so. Because all that makes my head hurt."

Heather laughed. "Marketing involves more numbers than people realize. I also thought we could organize another food fair and competition this summer, like the one you did before, Mom. It would be perfect timing with the cookbook launch."

Marina smiled. "These are all big steps. Let's take one at a time, sweetheart. I don't want to put any stress on your new marriage."

Listening to Heather's ideas, Ginger appreciated how far her family had come since Marina and Kai returned to Summer Beach. She was pleased to see Heather and her granddaughters enthusiastic about their work and lives.

Tapping her pencil, Marina said, "These are all intriguing, but let's not forget what we're here for today. We must make sure all the recipes are correct. And the layout needs to be gorgeous eye candy."

Ginger nodded in agreement. "Your first cookbook must be as good as it can be. Don't rush it."

Heather bit her lip. "You're right. There's still so much to do. What if we miss something? Or people don't like the recipes?"

"Don't worry. I'll make sure we don't make any mistakes." Marina reached out and squeezed her daughter's hand. "Many of these are our family recipes I tweaked for the cafe. Our customers love these dishes; you've said so yourself."

Heather shook out her hands. "I guess I am a little nervous about everything."

"That's normal stage fright," Kai said, sitting up. "Now that's something I know all about."

Laughter rippled around the table, and Heather let out a long sigh. Ginger enjoyed seeing them work together and support each other. They all had different talents.

They continued to discuss details about the cookbook, balancing their excitement with the need for perfection. Ginger was sure they were on the brink of another success that would expand the cafe business. She was pleased to be involved.

She could hardly wait to review the final edited manuscript and see the cover and book layout. As for Jack's book, as much as she had enjoyed working with him on it, she had shared all she cared to. He might not understand, but some things she preferred to keep private.

## 18

*G*inger felt the familiar burn in her calves as she and Jack ascended the winding trail to the ridgetop above Summer Beach. Unzipping her windbreaker, she paused to allow Jack to catch up.

"Not much farther now," she said, gesturing ahead.

"I know, we've done this before," Jack said, slightly out of breath. "Lead the way."

In her opinion, the view was worth every step. She felt on top of the world here, where anything seemed possible. This spot had been her refuge and source of strength and inspiration for years.

It wasn't a long hike, but it was steep in places. She skirted those areas for Jack and her knees. She could make the climb, take a short break to meditate, give thanks, or sort out problems, and be back at the cottage by breakfast.

However, Jack was not an early riser, so they were later today.

As they continued their climb, Ginger's mind wandered to the conversation she knew was coming. Jack had been persistent in his questioning about Sandi and Dennis, and she had a feeling today would be no different.

Finally, they crested the ridge. The village of Summer Beach sprawled out below them, a patchwork of neat streets and palm trees leading to the beach. Beyond, the vast expanse of the Pacific Ocean stretched to the horizon, its surface glittering like jewels in the morning sun.

"What a wonderful place to call home," she said, stretching her arms overhead.

To one side, a long row of estates lined the ridgetop. Clustered beneath them were Ginger's favorite spots in town: the Seabreeze Inn, Hidden Garden, Page's Bookshop, Beach Waves salon, and Nailed It hardware.

Gazing out, she saw brisk business at City Hall, the Seal Cove Inn, First Summer Beach Bank, and Louise's Laundry Basket.

Jack stood next to her, looking out. "Best day of my life when I found this town."

"Bertrand and I spent many exciting years away, but I was always happy to return."

Summer Beach was already busy. She saw the coffee crowd at Java Beach, and staff and diners entering the Starfish Cafe, Beaches, Rosa's Tacos, Spirits & Vine, and Mel's Fish. People milled around the Summer Beach marina, Seabreeze Shores community park, and Fisherman's Wharf.

"There is still a lot for me to discover here," Jack said. "Your family has been entrenched here for many years."

"The Delavie-Moore family has contributed its share to the town." She nodded, satisfied with what they'd accomplished here.

She spied Kai and Axe's Seashell outdoor amphitheater, her beloved Coral Cottage, and Marina's Coral Cafe with two food trucks now parked beside it. The farmers market where Brooke sold her produce and Marina's baked goods was busy, too.

"It's a breathtaking view from up here," Jack said. He shrugged off his lightweight jacket as the sun appeared from behind the marine layer.

"It's good to remember how our lives fit together." Ginger settled on a large outcropping of rock. "The vastness of the ocean gives proper perspective to our small challenges."

They sat in silence for a few moments before Jack cleared his throat. "I was hoping we could talk about your memories of Sandi and Dennis."

Ginger's heart clenched; she had dreaded recalling this part of the story. When she'd received the tragic news, she'd nearly broken down. But as she opened her mouth to speak, something held her back.

*Some memories are only for me*, she thought.

When she didn't respond, Jack asked, "What about Dennis's family?"

Ginger shook her head. "Sandi's husband was orphaned and raised in foster care. I was proud of the young man he turned out to be. Always seizing opportunities, studying hard to become an accountant, a certified public accountant, and then a corporate accountant. They married the summer after their first year at university. Too young, I thought, but then, I married at the same age, didn't I? Marina was born soon afterward."

"I've been thinking," she continued. "I don't believe we should include my recollections about Sandi and Dennis in the book."

Jack raised his eyebrows. "May I ask why?"

Ginger gazed out at the ocean, choosing her words carefully. "Let the past rest. My granddaughters wouldn't want the accident, or its aftermath, included."

"I can appreciate that it's a sensitive topic." He hesitated, scrubbing his face. "I hate to ask, but I have to. You and Bertrand were privy to classified information. Off the record and only between us, was it truly an accident? Or were there extenuating circumstances?"

Closing her eyes, Ginger recalled the detectives' gut-wrenching questions. "It was thoroughly investigated and proven strictly an accident. The roads were rain slicked, and conditions were treacherous." She shook her head. "It could have happened to anyone."

Jack picked up a small rock and turned it over in his hands. "Marina has shared a lot with me. What if I write that chapter based on what I know? You'll have full editorial approval. That goes for the entire manuscript as well."

Clasping her legs, she considered this option. "Do you think that would help others who might be having similarly difficult times?"

"With all due respect, I believe it would. That was a critical juncture in your life. You led the family through it, which likely required more mental toughness than breaking any code."

"You're right about that." She lifted her face to the sun,

relieved at his proposal. "Now, I prefer to enjoy my moments and look to the future."

Perhaps Oliver would be part of that future. They'd been speaking by phone almost every evening. She enjoyed having someone with a shared background and of a similar age to talk to again. Oliver wasn't Bertrand, but he was also intelligent and unique.

Jack picked up another smooth pebble. "It's what people do when faced with challenges that hone their character and inspire others. I promise I'll do this justice."

"Alright." She drew another deep breath with resolve. "Now that that's settled, shall we head back down?"

As they began their descent, coastal wildflowers nodded in the breeze as they passed, as if approving her decision. Consumed with thoughts, she didn't speak on the hike down. Jack, to his credit, respected her silence.

Reflecting, Ginger thought about the first heart-wrenching year after Sandi and Dennis passed away. She moved into the family home in Claremont, and Marina returned to university. The days passed in a blur.

After Brooke and Kai finished their school year, Ginger brought them to Summer Beach. By then, Marina had met Stan, a wonderful young man who eased her heartache. They married, and Ginger was happy they were starting a life together. Stan was a young officer in the military, while Marina studied and worked at a cafe.

However, their happiness was short-lived. Marina was pregnant with twins, and Stan lost his life in Afghanistan. She also returned to Summer Beach.

Soon, the cottage rang with the voices of Ginger's three granddaughters and Marina's newborns.

Jack knew all that. He would do fine, she decided.

Just then, his heel slid on the dirt path, and she caught his arm. "Be careful," she said. "One can fall quickly."

"So it seems," Jack said, looking sheepish. "What did you do when everything fell around you?"

"After the accident, I suddenly had to care for a growing family. I reached out to my former contacts and took on contract work in my fields of expertise. Many people I worked with before provided work."

That included Kurt, Grace, and Silas, among others. Even dear Oliver had referred her to people. She named them all for Jack.

"Are those some of the so-called vacation trips you still take?"

She smiled and nodded. "You figured that out, did you?"

"Marina wondered why she never met those friends or saw photos."

"I didn't want to worry anyone, and I can't share many details." She went on. "As you've heard, I also taught at the local high school."

"How could you do that without teaching credentials?"

She kicked a branch in the path to one side. "When the Summer Beach school board learned of my availability, they created a special visiting lecturer status for me so I could teach math. It worked for everyone."

By the time they reached the end of their hike, Ginger decided that Jack was right to include that part of her history.

If her story could serve others, that was all that mattered.

And that was the entire point of this manuscript.

Now, she thought of those chaotic days with tenderness. In Summer Beach, her family had healed together, finally finding sunshine on the other side of the storm.

———

GINGER STOOD at the kitchen counter of her cottage. She had just returned from a vigorous swim in the ocean with her middle granddaughter. Brooke excelled on the swim team in high school. After their ocean swim, Brooke quickly showered and left on a date with Chip, a newly minted firefighter in a community south of Summer Beach.

Ginger liked Chip, even though he was still a boy at heart. Brooke had an earth mother presence, and the two were good together.

With all the girls busy, the soothing sound of waves crashing on the shore was her only company. The setting sun cast a warm pink glow through the windows. She looked out, enjoying the moment. They'd come so far in the last year.

Tonight, she was making a light supper of salad, French onion soup, and sandwiches from a roasted chicken she'd prepared the day before—just as her friend in Cambridge had taught her so many years ago. These days, she loved watching Julia's cooking show on television.

This dinner was only for herself and Marina, who had just put the twins down to sleep. Kai had her first theater rehearsal at school in a lead role she'd been thrilled to land. A neighbor would bring her home later.

Marina entered the kitchen with excitement etched on her face. "I have some news," she began, her voice tinged with nervous energy.

"What is it, dear?"

"I've been offered a job in San Francisco," Marina blurted out, her eyes shining. "It's with a television station. I also found an *au pair* to help with the twins."

Ginger's heart swelled with pride and a touch of concern. Marina had been working toward finding a job for months. "That's wonderful news," she said, pulling her into a warm embrace. "You've earned this."

As they sat down at the small kitchen table, Ginger studied Marina's face. "I'm happy for you, but I want to make sure you're ready for this. It's been quite a year for you, adjusting to motherhood—and everything else."

Determination was evident in Marina's eyes. "It's time for me to figure out my life. This job has upward mobility, and it pays well. I can't rely on you forever."

Ginger reached across the table, squeezing Marina's hand. "You know I don't mind, sweetheart. I'm happy to help for as long as you need."

"I know, and I'm so grateful," Marina replied. "But you've done so much already. You've been supporting all of us—me with the twins, Kai with her acting and dance, even helping Brooke and Chip get settled in San Diego."

Ginger nodded, thinking of Brooke, who was planning her wedding. They were already talking about starting a family. "Brooke and Chip will be fine. And Kai has found a new passion. Are you sure you won't stay?"

"It's time for me to find my path, too. The twins are a

year old, and I'm ready for this next step. San Francisco will be new and exciting. Someday, I could be a morning news anchor and still have time to pick up the kids from school."

Clearly, Marina had thought this out. Ginger was proud of her for taking a chance. Her granddaughters were growing up and finding their way in the world despite tragedy. That was the mark of character.

With Marina leaving, Brooke could look after Kai if Ginger had to travel for an engagement, as she would in the summer after school let out. Those assignments paid well, allowing her to do all she wanted for her granddaughters and the little twins. Bertrand's retirement was adequate for her, but she needed to help the girls. And she enjoyed doing it.

"This calls for a celebration," Ginger said. "I'm so proud of you, darling."

As they chatted about the details of Marina's new job and the upcoming move, Ginger felt a sense of deep satisfaction. She had stepped in to support her granddaughters through the most difficult time of their lives.

Each young woman was finding her way to a bright future. Marina and Brooke were following their paths, and young Kai's goal was to audition for summer stock and commercials next year. She was so naturally talented that Ginger immediately gave her approval.

As her family moved forward, Ginger vowed to support them however she could.

Finishing the dinner preparations, she glanced around her kitchen. This home had seen many changes since Bertrand had surprised her with it on their wedding day.

Someday, the girls would all gather here with their children to play on the beach, just as she had as a child. She
smiled at the thought as she and Marina carried their dishes
to the patio to eat and relax.

## 19

*M*arina was tidying the cafe, and Cruise was cooking when Blake arrived for a late lunch, as he often did to see Heather.

"Have a seat at the family table here in the kitchen," Marina told him. "It's slowing down now, and Heather will want to eat with you." She enjoyed having him here, and they were so sweet together.

Blake slid onto the bench. "I've been dreaming about those blackened salmon sliders you were testing."

"You're in luck," Marina said. "We just added them to the menu."

"Hey man, I can whip those up for you," Cruise said, bumping fists with Blake.

"Hi, honey." Heather swept into the kitchen and gave Blake a peck on the cheek. "I just closed out my last table, so we can talk about our engagement party plans until I need to start studying for my exam."

"I'm open to ideas," Marina said, brushing crumbs from her kitchen jacket.

"Ginger mentioned an elegant soiree at Hidden Garden, but we're thinking of a beach barbecue," Heather said, her eyes sparkling with pleasure. "Something simple and easy. Mom, I don't want you or Aunt Kai or Ginger to go to any trouble planning this. We're all super busy."

Blake nodded. "Most of my friends are nearby. We figured we could set up a volleyball net and have a lot of fun."

"Whatever you two want," Marina said. "Ginger will understand. When were you thinking of having it?"

Heather glanced at Blake before answering. "We were hoping to do it before the holiday rush. Maybe in a couple of weeks? The weather will be warm enough, and the date won't clash with Thanksgiving or Christmas holidays. That's another reason to keep it simple."

Marina nodded, already thinking of possibilities. "That's a good idea. We could close the cafe early that day and use it as a base for cooking and preparations. It would be much easier than trying to transport everything to the beach. People can eat here on the patio."

"Put me down for grill duty," Cruise said.

"We sure appreciate that," Blake said. "If it's not too much trouble."

Heather gave Cruise a high five. "Maybe Aunt Kai could give us some decorating ideas. I don't want her to do too much. How is she doing?"

"She's feeling better," Marina said, wiping the counter. "Her tests came back normal, and the doctor told her that feeling tired is a normal part of pregnancy. Now that she's taking naps, she's bounced back like the Tigger we all know. Leo's care basket sure brightened her spirits."

"That was so sweet of him," Heather added.

Blake's phone rang, and he glanced down. "I must take this call. We brought in some seal pups that were injured. I need to make sure they're doing okay."

After Blake excused himself, Heather turned back to Marina. "I should warn you. Blake invited his mother, but his father told everyone he plans to boycott the engagement party and the wedding. I'm afraid Blake will be hurt."

Marina considered her words carefully. "Maybe that's for the best."

"His mother said if his father shows up, she'll leave." Heather asked, "What should I do?"

"Just talk to Blake and be supportive," Marina advised gently. "He knows his parents best. If there is an issue, you can stand united. I don't think Blake will let his father ruin your wedding."

Heather nodded, absorbing her mother's advice. "You're right. Thanks, Mom."

"Establish boundaries with his father early because when you marry Blake, you'll have a relationship with his entire family, for better or worse."

Heather sucked in a breath. "I'll work on that."

When Blake returned, his face lit with a smile at the sight of Heather, and Marina felt a surge of protective love for her daughter. She hoped that whatever was causing the tension with Blake's parents could be resolved.

Still, Heather was quite capable now. Since moving to Summer Beach, her daughter had grown out of her timid phase and blossomed. In high school, Heather tended to lean on Ethan, the gregarious one of them. Now, with her brother following his path and traveling to golf tournaments, Heather had found herself and developed her voice.

Blake seemed good for her as he encouraged her even more.

Marina picked up a pencil and a tablet to take notes as Heather and Blake talked. "We'll need to plan and order food. How many of your San Francisco friends do you want to invite? We also need to reserve rooms at the Seabreeze Inn and the Seal Cove Inn for out-of-town guests."

While Heather launched into a preliminary guest list, Marina made a note to call Blake's mother again. She hoped Arlette would be more receptive without her husband.

Heather suddenly stopped. "Who is that going to the Coral Cottage?"

An older, trim man with white hair left his vintage Jaguar convertible by the house and walked toward the front door. He walked briskly and wore upscale casual clothes as if he were going out to dinner.

Marina put her pencil down and craned her neck. "I've never seen that man before."

Just then, he snapped his fingers and turned around. He bent to retrieve something from the car.

"Flowers!" Heather clamped a hand to her face in surprise. "What's going on, Mom? Is Ginger dating someone?"

Marina was just as surprised as her daughter was. "People take each other flowers for all sorts of events. Like..." She couldn't think of anything.

"Maybe someone died," Cruise offered.

"Shh," Marina said, waving a hand. "He looks too happy for that."

As if he'd heard them, the man turned around.

Instinctively, they all looked away, busying themselves.

"Okay, he's going in," Heather said, peeking again. "I should go over there, just in case he has the wrong house."

Blake chuckled. "Ginger can probably manage that, honey."

"But she's there by herself," Heather said. "What if the flowers are some sort of cover?"

Cruise turned around. "I think she could probably take him. Jack was limping yesterday after Ginger took him on one of her hikes up to the ridgetop."

So that's what happened to him. Marina tossed her cleaning rag into the sink. "I'll go." She scooped some muffins into a carry-out box. "I'll say she wanted these."

"I'm coming, too." Heather grabbed Blake's hand. "If he's dangerous, we'll need you."

"Oh, for heaven's sake," Marina said. "Don't you think we look a little obvious?"

The three of them set off, leaving Cruise chuckling behind them.

Marina went through the rear door. "Hi, Ginger. I brought some muffins from the cafe. We had a lot left over, and I know you wanted them." She left the muffins in the kitchen and stopped at the entry to the living room where Ginger and the man were standing. "Oh, hello. I hope I'm not intruding."

Heather and Blake were right behind her.

"It's a day for gifts, it seems." Ginger smiled and took the flowers. "I feel like it's my birthday. Girls—and Blake, why, what a surprise. I'd like you all to meet Oliver Powell, a dear friend I've known most of my life, although we only recently reconnected."

"I'm pleased to meet you all," Oliver said with an engaging smile.

"I just wanted Blake to help me with something upstairs," Heather said, stumbling over her words. "I-I wanted to look at your wedding dress."

That surprised Marina, and she saw Ginger's eyes light with happiness.

"It can wait." Blake greeted Oliver and shook hands with him. "Very nice to meet you, sir."

Ginger explained how they were all related, and Oliver looked interested.

"Hello, Marina," he said, greeting her. "I see so much of your mother in you. And Ginger, of course."

"You knew my mother?" Marina hadn't expected that, and it took her by surprise.

"Oh, yes," Oliver said. "Sandi was a sweet, lovely young woman. She was the center of Ginger and Bertrand's world."

Ginger placed a hand on his forearm and smiled. "Oliver and his brother Kurt were very good friends to Bertrand and me. Kurt hired me for my first job."

The name clicked in Marina's memory. "The celebration of life you attended. That was for Kurt, wasn't it?" When Oliver nodded, she expressed her condolences. "I'm so sorry for your loss."

Oliver thanked her. "Kurt lived a wonderful life, and his last act was to reconnect me with Ginger."

"My goodness, wouldn't that have made him happy?"

Ginger pressed a hand to her chest. "I wish he'd known I came to his last party."

Oliver's lively blue eyes crinkled at the corners with amusement. "Oh, but he did. Kurt planned the guest list and made me promise to invite you. He really did bring us together again."

Marina sensed the attraction between them. She hadn't seen Ginger show interest in anyone since their grandfather passed away, and that was decades ago. And that lovely dress Ginger wore—Marina had never seen it before.

Suddenly, she felt embarrassed. They were intruding.

"If you'll excuse us, we're needed at the cafe." Marina extended her hand to Oliver. "It's been so nice to meet you, Oliver. I hope we'll see more of you in Summer Beach."

Oliver raised an eyebrow at Ginger, who smiled demurely at that. "Maybe you will," he replied, sounding hopeful. "Likewise, it's been a pleasure meeting you all."

When they burst through the back door, Marina let out a breath. "I can't believe we just crashed Ginger's first date in decades." She turned and came face to face with Jack.

"You did what?" he asked.

"Uh-oh, I think Cruise needs me," Heather said. "And Blake, your order must be ready." She grabbed his hand.

Jack watched them go, shaking his head. "Are you going to tell me what's going on?"

"Well, sure, but why are you here?" Marina felt flustered, like she'd been caught sneaking around. Which she supposed she had been.

He folded his arms. "Because we're married, and sometimes I like to see you. When you're not snooping into your grandmother's business."

She kissed him. "We were just checking on her." Quickly, she told him what happened. "But don't put that in the book."

"It's off the record unless she tells me otherwise." Jack sighed, threw his arm around her, and they returned to the kitchen. "Does Blake know what he's getting into with this family?"

Blake and Heather looked up from their salmon sliders with guilty expressions.

"If you know what's good for you, you'll let that be a surprise," Marina said, nudging him. They all laughed, and then she whispered to Heather, "Did you mean that about Ginger's wedding dress?"

This time, Heather's eyes lit with delight. "I'd love to wear it. Size-wise, I'm sort of in between you and Aunt Kai. Do you think Ginger would let me?"

Marina hugged her daughter. "I could tell she loved the idea. But it's bad luck for the groom to see it before the wedding."

Heather chuckled at that. "Uh, Mom? It's in your wedding photos all over the house."

"Well, don't tell him that," Marina said. "How about I hide the photos when Blake comes over?"

"Too late for that." Jack chuckled and shook his head. "Blake, you're in for a wild ride and the best time of your life, buddy. Welcome to the family."

"Look, there they go," Heather whispered, nodding toward Ginger and Oliver. He opened the car door for her. "I mean, don't look."

Marina laughed and turned back to work. Although her grandmother might deny having an interest in Oliver, her actions indicated otherwise.

Jack joined Heather and Blake, and Marina started lunch for him. The familiar rhythms of the cafe surrounded her—the clinking of dishes, the hum of conversation, the aromas of the kitchen—but her mind was elsewhere. She could hardly wait to see Ginger and tease out more details about Oliver.

Ginger might insist there was nothing between them; she might wave away Marina's questions with an elegant hand, but Marina knew better.

She'd seen the spark in Ginger's eyes and noticed the new dress she had on—and the earrings she saved for special occasions. Her actions gave her away.

Marina couldn't be happier for her. If anyone deserved a second chance at love, it was her remarkable grandmother. She'd never thought about it because Ginger was so self-sufficient.

A warm glow gathered in her chest as she plated Jack's sliders. She had the feeling Ginger's life had more interesting chapters to come.

## 20

"What a well-preserved car," Ginger said as she settled into the buttery leather seat of Oliver's vintage Jaguar convertible.

The car purred to life under Oliver's touch. "I like quality, and I take care of things I love." He looked at her as he spoke, his meaning clear.

She smiled and tied a yellow Italian silk scarf over her hair. He was full of compliments, but she didn't mind. It had been so long since she'd enjoyed this sort of banter and attention.

"Ready for an adventure?" Oliver's eyes twinkled beneath the brim of the jaunty driving cap he'd donned.

"Always." Still, a flutter arose in her chest that had nothing to do with the car's vibration. That was most unlike her.

Not that she'd forgotten how that felt.

As they pulled away from the Coral Cottage, Ginger

caught a glimpse of Marina and the others sneaking glances their way. She smiled, imagining the excited chatter among them.

"I thought we'd take a brisk drive before dinner. It's such a gorgeous day." Oliver turned on the heater and maneuvered the Jaguar onto the coastal highway.

The warmth kept Ginger toasty against the brisk wind off the ocean as they whipped along the coast. The drive felt exhilarating, and she remembered doing this with Bertrand. "You're an expert driver."

Oliver grinned. "I had my share of races back in the day."

"You were such a daredevil then."

"I sure was." He chuckled as he followed the curve in the road. "My risk-taking is more calculated now."

Ginger adjusted her sunglasses and let that comment slide. Or maybe he hadn't meant it that way. She was out of practice on the courtship scene.

"This reminds me of driving along the Côte d'Azur with Bertrand," Ginger mused, letting the memories wash over her.

Oliver nodded with a wistful smile. "Margaret and I had a similar car in Buenos Aires. She always said it made her feel like a movie star."

"She was such a sweet friend," Ginger said.

"And you got lucky with Bertrand."

"What wonderful times we've had." Remembering the good times and focusing on possibilities was a choice she made every day. That's why she chose not to relive parts of her life with Jack.

"And a few heartaches," Oliver added.

She touched his shoulder. "Yes, but the rewards are worth it. One must come to terms with heartaches and move on. If I am defined at all, let it be by my contributions, not my sorrows."

"Who said that?"

Ginger laughed. "I just did."

"You're a treasure, Ginger." They chatted easily, and after a few minutes, Oliver turned on an old tune. "Remember this?"

Ella Fitzgerald's voice rang out in *Misty*. "I loved this," Ginger said, humming along. "I'm surprised you remembered."

The music and their laughter mingled with the sound of crashing waves. As they drove, the initial awkwardness of a first date at their age melted away, replaced by the comfortable camaraderie of old friends embarking on a new chapter.

At a lull in the conversation, Oliver asked, "Do you travel as much as you did?"

"I still consult on the East Coast, though not as much. Occasionally, I take a trip with a friend, but I haven't traveled like Bertrand and I once did. What about you?"

"I went on a tour a few months ago to the Amazon rainforest. The tour was interesting but going alone was not for me." He glanced at her with genuine interest. "What's next on your travel bucket list?"

"I've been dreaming of returning to Paris. There used to be a little patisserie near the U.S. Embassy that made the best *pain au chocolat*. I wonder if it's still there."

"Maybe we could find out together some time," Oliver ventured.

"We'll see," Ginger replied with a small smile.

A self-conscious grin touched his face. "I'm being too forward, aren't I?"

"Just a little, but it's sweet." She enjoyed the harmless flirtation. "What's on your travel list?"

"I'd like to visit new places and experience new sights. Maybe the markets of Marrakech, or the wildlife of the Serengeti."

"Sounds exciting. Where else have you been that you loved?"

"So many places, and I've appreciated each one," Oliver replied. As he drove, he regaled her with tales of his adventures in Europe and South America.

Ginger loved hearing his stories. She was captivated not only by those but also by the man. He'd run a global advertising business for years. His enthusiasm for life was infectious, his wit sharp and engaging. And his memory was as good as hers.

"For two octogenarians," Ginger said, a mischievous glint in her eye, "we're certainly not acting our age."

Oliver threw his head back in laughter. "Never act your age; it's only a number. A person's zest for living is what counts. And you've got that, Ginger."

The sun dipped lower on the horizon as they continued their drive. They stopped at a small cove and talked more while watching the sun set, never running out of wide-ranging topics that interested them.

Renewed possibilities for the future emerged in Ginger's mind. Here she was, embarking on what felt like a new adventure. The road ahead was uncertain, but with Oliver by her side and the wind in her hair, Ginger wondered if the best was yet to come.

"I have dinner reservations at Beaches restaurant near you," he said. "Will that suit you?"

"They have an excellent chef," she replied, nodding. "It's quite upscale for the beach, but who doesn't enjoy good food in a beautiful atmosphere?"

"I'll add fascinating companionship to that, too," he replied.

On their return trip, the conversation continued to flow easily between them. The sunset dusted the sky with gold.

Finally, they arrived at Beaches, one of Ginger's favorite restaurants with the best ocean view in town.

"That drive was marvelous," Ginger said. Feeling exhilarated, she removed her scarf and fluffed her hair.

Oliver watched her. "I'm glad you enjoyed it. I thought you might."

After they were seated at a table, Ginger found herself studying Oliver's face, noting the laugh lines around his eyes and the distinguished silver of his hair.

They ordered Chef Marguerite's special seafood medley. When the server asked if they would like wine, Ginger said to Oliver, "You probably have a long drive."

"I'm staying at the Seabreeze Inn tonight. We can enjoy a glass. And I think I remember what you like."

"Let's see if you do," she said, issuing a mild challenge. But he did, so she would have lost that bet. The server delivered the *amuse-bouche* and two robust Bordeaux wines to the table.

"Why are you staying overnight? Not that I mind," she added.

"I thought I would look around." Oliver sipped his wine, watching her reaction. "Maybe find a place to rent. I've already been in touch with a local real estate agent. Summer Beach is a very welcoming community."

"It's a wonderful place. I hope you find something that suits you." She realized she meant that.

"What keeps you busy here?"

"When I'm in town, I volunteer at the senior center, teaching computer skills. And then there's the Coral Cafe," Ginger continued. "I helped Marina start it by contributing my guest cottage. We've had such fun, and it's become a popular spot in town. She's enormously talented."

"What about your other granddaughters?"

"I have been abundantly fortunate." She spoke with pride about Kai's acting and directing, as well as Brooke's gardening and family. Ethan, Heather, and Brooke's children—she was proud of each of them. Then she shared the children's books series she and Jack collaborated on and their latest project, her biography.

"My word, Ginger," Oliver said, clearly impressed. "You don't have time to be lonely, do you?"

"Time is a resource, and like all my resources, I use it wisely."

Oliver looked at her with interest. "You haven't changed at all."

"Oh, no. We all do," Ginger said. "Every day, hundreds of billions of cells in our body are replaced. We can and do change daily."

"Then I have no excuse." A wistful smile touched his lips.

Over dinner, they shared more stories and laughter, thoroughly enjoying themselves. Yet, Ginger detected an undercurrent of tension. The possibility of what might develop loomed between them.

After their meal, Ginger felt Oliver's gaze on her. She decided to be direct, which was generally the best course of action between two intelligent people, she'd found. "Tell me what's on your mind, Oliver."

He chuckled. "With all that you do, I wonder if you have room in your life for a relationship?"

The question hung in the air between them. *There it is*, she thought, reminded of Bertrand's sensible proposal so many years ago. Oliver was not unlike him.

He had a valid point. She hadn't considered what having a man in her life might entail, mainly because she hadn't met any she was remotely interested in.

"Your real question is not one, but two. First, do I have room for a relationship, and second, do I want a deeper relationship with you?"

Oliver smiled at her grasp of his question.

"We make room for what's important to us," she said. "That includes relationships, if those are worthy of us. What about you, Oliver?"

His face colored lightly. "You've already figured me out."

She touched his hand as the server stopped to check on them. After the server filled their water glasses and left, Ginger changed direction. She wasn't ready to commit to an answer. "Surely, you fill your life with interesting activities."

"Did Bertrand's diplomatic skills rub off on you, or was it the other way around?" Oliver smiled. "I can't remember when I've had such a fascinating conversation. But to answer your question, I play golf and manage my investments. I coached a Little League baseball team until they grew up. But considering my billions of new cells every day, I should explore new frontiers."

She respected that.

After they finished their meal, Oliver reached across the table and gently took her hand. "I've had a wonderful time tonight. I'd like to see you again, if you're up for it?"

Ginger considered this, projecting the array of future outcomes. A large part of her wanted to say yes immediately, while another part hesitated.

She'd been alone so long.

"I've enjoyed myself, too," she said. "Perhaps we should take some time to think about what we both want. And go slower."

Oliver nodded, understanding in his eyes. "As you wish."

They left the restaurant, and Ginger found herself at a crossroads. The familiarity of her busy, independent life was comfortable and known. Yet, the idea of companionship and new adventures with Oliver was a fascinating new variable in the equation of life. Was she ready to risk her heart again?

Oliver pulled the car in front of her cottage and opened her door.

Taking his hand, she slid out. "Thank you for a lovely evening."

Oliver leaned in, placing a gentle kiss on her cheek. "I'll think about what you said. Above all, I hope we'll always be friends."

His lips were soft and warm on her cheek, stirring her feelings for him. "Friendship is the basis for the best relationships," she said before closing her eyes and taking a leap of faith. She kissed him softly, and when she drew back, she saw unmistakable joy in his eyes. "On second thought, let's see where this goes."

Oliver embraced her. "Slowly, of course."

Inside, from the kitchen window, she watched him drive away. She could still feel his arms around her and the love that emanated from him. In that moment, she knew her world had shifted.

While she was out for her walk the following day, Oliver left a message. When she returned his call, he answered, sounding happy and upbeat. "Have you been looking for places in Summer Beach?" she asked.

"I looked at three," he replied. "And I just leased a bungalow near the beach and your cottage."

Ginger was delighted. "Having you nearby will be convenient."

"I can walk to the Coral Cafe for coffee. Would you mind that?"

"If that question includes an invitation, I'd like that very much." She smiled to herself. The thought of starting her day with him made her surprisingly happy.

.  .  .

For the next few weeks, Ginger met Oliver nearly every morning at the cafe for breakfast. Marina and Heather became accustomed to seeing him there, and they developed a rapport with Oliver. He also got along well with Jack and Blake, and she was pleased to hear them asking him for advice.

Today was Heather and Blake's engagement party. Kai and Marina were organizing the event, so Kai's snappy show tunes were blasting from Heather's room, where they were helping her get ready. Ginger would miss Heather being here, but with the cafe a short walk away, she could still see her every day.

Ginger dressed in a mid-length floral dress with a mustard-colored pashmina shawl wrapped around her shoulders. She had invited Oliver, too. The party would be their first family event together. She looped a strand of pink coral around her neck, added a sheen of pink lipstick, and clipped her ginger-tinted hair back with soft tendrils around her face.

When she heard Oliver's car, she started downstairs. On her way, she thought about their evolving life—their walks on the beach, hikes in the hills, and even their joint presentation at the senior center. Oliver had impressed her with his financial expertise, complementing her computer skills without overshadowing her. It felt like a true partnership, much as she'd had before.

"Hello, darling," Ginger said, kissing him lightly at the door. "I thought we should arrive early to help."

Behind them, a commotion erupted on the stairs as Heather, Kai, and Marina came downstairs.

"Let's go fly a kite," Kai sang, twirling around, holding her belly.

Ginger laughed and clapped. "She's considering putting on *Mary Poppins* at the theater next summer for the little tykes of Summer Beach. Although, I'd like it, too."

Oliver kicked up his heels to one side. "If you need a grandpa, I'm available."

"Why, Oliver," Ginger cried. "What an impressive move."

"Be careful," Kai said, twirling a finger at him. "Keep that up, and I'll cast you."

"She's not kidding," Heather added. "We've all been drafted into Kai's plays. The Christmas show still needs extras."

"Are you in it?" Oliver asked Ginger.

"I enjoy being the announcer. Marina and I will trade off this year. You're welcome to sit in with me."

"I'd like that," he said. "You're full of endless surprises, my dear."

Heather's phone buzzed. "Blake is waiting for us at the cafe. And his mother just arrived."

"Let's go," Ginger said, embracing Heather. "You look perfectly radiant."

She recalled the small engagement party she'd had in Summer Beach at her parent's home many years ago.

Recently, Arlette had joined Ginger, Marina, and Heather for lunch. Without her husband, Arlette was kind and happy to meet them. She'd told them how relieved she was that Blake had met Heather, taking the pressure off him to acquiesce to his father's demands. She told them she and Ken were separated but going through counseling with the hope of saving their marriage.

As they made their way to the cafe, Ginger delighted in its transformation. Marina and Heather had turned it into a romantic beach wonderland for the engagement party. Even Leo had helped.

Stacks of kites, frisbees, sunscreen, and beach towels on a long table drew attention. Some of Heather's local friends, including Sunny and Poppy from the Seabreeze Inn, had also strung a volleyball net on the beach for the occasion. Gift bags printed with *Heather & Blake* glittered by the gift table. Beach music played in the background, putting everyone in a light-hearted mood.

Blake's voice rang out above the gathering crowd. "Hey, sweetheart, over here."

Heather rushed to him, her face glowing with happiness.

Ginger noted the adoration in his eyes as he gazed at Heather. "He looks at her with such love. I know they're a good match."

With a smile, Oliver caught her hand. "You're a fine judge of relationships."

"I like to think so," she said, touching his cheek. "And there is no one I'd rather have by my side than you."

As they mingled with the guests, Ginger noticed Arlette, Blake's mother, standing awkwardly by the buffet.

"Excuse me," Marina said. "I'll join Arlette."

Brooke and her family joined them. "You look so lovely, Ginger." She, Chip, and their three sons greeted them with hugs before Chip sent the boys off to fetch lemonade for Ginger and Oliver.

"Good to see you both," Chip said, shaking Oliver's hand. "Jack told me you like to golf. There's an excellent public course not far from here. You're welcome to join me sometime."

Oliver looked pleased. "I'd sure like that, thanks."

Ginger noticed the ease with which they included Oliver and expected his presence at family gatherings. Seeing how her family was adapting to this new dynamic warmed her heart.

She accepted a glass of raspberry lemonade from her eldest great-grandson, currently in high school. Sipping the refreshing drink, Ginger surveyed the patio. Marina bustled around, introducing Arlette and ensuring everyone had cool libations and food. Heather and Blake greeted their guest with hugs and laughter.

The beach party lasted until dusk, with rousing games of volleyball. Jack drafted Oliver into one game, and Ginger flew kites on the beach with Leo and Brooke's sons, Alder, Rowan, and Oakley.

Many of the guests left, but the family and a few close friends remained, gathered around the firepit on the cafe patio.

Ginger and Oliver sat a little apart, relaxing and watching the continued shenanigans. She enjoyed being with him. He had a steady presence she was growing increasingly fond of.

Oliver wrapped his arms around her, and she leaned against him.

"What a perfect event," he said. "I'm pleased for Heather and Blake. And I appreciate being part of this."

"Everyone likes you."

Oliver chuckled at that. "You sound surprised."

"Why, not at all." She shrugged. "Well, maybe a little. My family can be quite protective of me, so I was concerned they might not accept you. But you won them over. You're practically part of the family now."

"That makes me very happy." Oliver kissed her cheek.

"Me, too," Ginger said, smoothing a hand over his shoulder.

They had talked about how Oliver and Margaret missed having children, but they were close to their nieces and nephews. One nephew had already visited him in Summer Beach, and Ginger looked forward to meeting more of them.

Having known each other for many years, they had quickly fallen into step with each other. They'd already talked about keeping their homes, at least for now. They each liked having their space, although they spent a great deal of time together.

"Ginger Delavie," Oliver said, shaking his head in amazement. "I feel like the luckiest man in the world these days."

Feeling close to him, she kissed his hand. "We have your brother Kurt to thank for playing matchmaker."

He chuckled at that. "For you, not once, but twice."

She realized that was true. "We're so fortunate to have another chance at companionship."

"And love," Oliver added, lifting a strand of hair from her forehead.

"Yes," she agreed, with all the happiness in her heart. "And love. We have so much to look forward to."

"More stories, laughter, and memories to make," Oliver said. "Our first holiday season together and trips to plan."

A thought crossed her mind and she smiled. "Jack might have to add another chapter to the manuscript."

For the first time in years, Ginger was excited about the prospect of romance. She looked forward to a new phase of life with Oliver with all the joy in her heart.

"My dear, dear friend," she said, raising her face to his. "I seem to have fallen in love with you."

Against the flickering flames of the firepit, Oliver kissed her. "And I've fallen for you all over again."

# EPILOGUE

"Fresh blueberry, cranberry orange, and banana nut muffins," Ginger said to passersby as she spread Marina's baked goods on the table at the farmers market. Aromas of fresh produce, flowers, and baked goods filled the air.

The holidays had passed with plenty of celebrations, including her first Christmas and New Year with Oliver.

Now, the snowbirds were returning to Summer Beach. The market was already busy.

Brooke was running late this morning because one of the boys had been ill last night. With Chip away on a long shift at the fire station, she had to pick up medication before she left. She had called Marina to see if she would set up the food stall for her.

Ginger also volunteered to help. She turned to Marina. "Have you seen Kai?"

"Not yet, but she should be here. She usually shops for

produce early." Marina sliced samples of bread, muffins, and cookies.

"Those muffins look delicious," one woman said, pausing at the table.

Marina offered her a tray of assorted samples. "Have a taste."

"It's an old family recipe," Ginger said. "You'll find it in my granddaughter's upcoming cookbook, *The Sunny Coast Table*, which is available for preorder now. Marina owns the Coral Cafe."

"I've heard of that," the woman said. "We've just returned to our beach house. Last year, I bought organic vegetables from Brooke. Will she be in today?"

"Soon," Ginger assured her. "Be sure to come back."

After the woman made her selections, Marina wrapped up her order and tucked a bookmark inside. The preorder page was live, and people were already placing orders.

"I hope Oakley feels better today," Marina said, putting out more breads and muffins.

Ginger agreed. "I'm sure Brooke will be here soon enough." She usually picked up the baked items from the cafe because Marina was busy prepping food and serving the morning crowd. Fortunately, Marina left Cruise in the kitchen with Heather and a new server she was training as her replacement.

Marina looked up. "Here's Kai now. And Brooke is right behind with her veggies."

"I was starting to worry about you," Ginger said to Kai, walking to the front of the stall to greet her. "How are you feeling?"

"I'm tired. I couldn't sleep last night." Kai rubbed her back.

Brooke wheeled in her produce in a wagon. "Thanks for covering for me. I still have a truckload to bring in." Catching sight of Kai, she frowned. "Kai, sweetheart, what's wrong?"

"My back is so sore it was impossible to get comfortable last night. This morning, I stood in a hot shower forever, but it hasn't helped. It's getting worse. And I've got some weird muscle cramps going on. This kiddo is two weeks late, and I'm getting tired of her mischief and acrobatics. We're going to have a heart-to-heart talk when she arrives."

"Show me where you're sore." Frowning with concern, Brooke placed her hand where Kai pointed and nodded. "Those might be contractions, and you could be in early labor. You should call your doctor now to see if you should go to the hospital. Have Axe meet you there."

Kai's eyes grew wide. "I tried him a few minutes ago, but he's on a job site outside of town that doesn't have good reception. What am I going to do?"

"Marina and I can take you." Ginger took Kai's arm, steadying her. "Deep breaths, darling. Let's go somewhere quiet to call your doctor."

"Do you think it's really time?" Kai asked, sucking in a panicked breath.

"You are overdue," Brooke said gently.

"I thought Axe would be with me. We had everything planned." Kai gripped her sisters' hands. "Please come with me, Brooke. You're the one with the most experience at this. I can't do this without you."

Brooke hugged her. "I'll unload the truck while you call

your doctor. If she tells you to come in, I'll have Cookie cover our spot, and I'll meet you at the hospital."

"Thank you," Kai whispered, hugging her.

As Ginger guided Kai to a nearby bench, her grand-daughter began shaking. She knew Kai's earlier health concerns were adding to her anxiety.

"I'm not ready," Kai said, easing onto the bench. "I thought I was, but what if something goes wrong?" With trembling hands, she called her doctor and explained how she felt. After a few moments, she hung up. "She told me to come now."

Ginger exchanged a glance with Marina, who was already pulling out her phone to call Axe.

Turning back to Kai, Ginger put her arm around her. "You've discussed all the possibilities with your doctor. Everything points to a safe delivery."

Ginger could feel the tension knotted in Kai's shoulders. "Remember your breathing classes? Let's do that together now. And Marina, bring the car closer. We'll meet you at the exit."

"Right away. I'll try Axe, too." Marina sprinted off.

The busy market faded into the background as Ginger focused on Kai, helping her through the breathing exercises to stay as calm as possible.

"Relax, and take your time," Ginger said, guiding Kai toward the exit. "Remember, deep breaths."

Kai quirked a worried grin. "I'm trying, but I feel like I have a basketball under my ribs."

Ginger smiled at her. "Listen to you, cracking jokes. We're almost there."

Marina parked her Mini Cooper steps from the exit and opened the door.

"Any luck reaching Axe?" Ginger asked.

Shaking her head, Marina replied, "The call keeps dropping."

Slowing to get into the car, Kai groaned. "What if he doesn't make it in time?"

"We'll reach him, and he'll be with you soon," Ginger assured her. "First babies usually take time to arrive."

Kai's eyes flew wide again. "Will I have time to get my bag at home?"

"We're going straight to the hospital, dear." Although earlier tests were fine, Ginger knew the physician was concerned that complications could develop.

Huffing, Kai squeezed into the small car. "Why aren't you driving an SUV?"

"I'll be sure to get one next time you're pregnant," Marina replied.

Kai frowned at her. "Why do you sound like you're enjoying this?"

"I'm sorry, and I promise I'm not," Marina said, glancing at Ginger. "If it's any comfort to you, imagine what having twins was like."

Pulling her legs into the car, Kai made a face. "Please don't remind me that they run in the family. I might never do this again." Biting her lip, she said, "I'm a little scared."

"You've got this," Marina said. "You once told me that you still have a sliver of fear before you go onstage, but you do it anyway. You said it's not about being fearless but knowing you're ready to perform and willing the outcome you desire."

"I guess I did say that." Kai gave her a weak grin.

While Marina steered toward the hospital, Ginger's phone buzzed. It was Brooke, her voice tinged with excitement. "How's Kai doing?"

Ginger eased into the back seat. "She's doing fine, but please meet us at the hospital. She needs you."

Ginger had supported Sandi, Marina, and Brooke during their deliveries, but Kai was particularly excitable. With Brooke's calm demeanor and experience, she would be a soothing presence for Kai.

After they arrived at the Summer Beach hospital, the staff quickly decided Kai was in labor and should stay.

Just then, Ginger's phone rang; it was Oliver. She usually met him at the cafe, so he was probably concerned. Quickly, she answered and explained.

"What can I do?" he asked.

She told him that they couldn't reach Axe. "Would you call his office manager, find out where he is, and go get him if you have to?"

"Leave it to me, love," he replied.

Ginger and Marina stayed with Kai as much as they were allowed. Finally, Brooke arrived.

Kai looked relieved to see her and gripped her arm. "I don't understand what's going on."

Brooke smoothed a hand over Kai's forehead. "I'll translate the medical speak for you. Your job is to relax and go with the flow. You have a good team caring for you. Remember, your doctor delivered my first baby."

Ginger was also relieved when Brooke suggested she and Marina take a break. She told them it would likely be a long day.

206 | JAN MORAN

Ginger and Marina walked downstairs for coffee and breakfast. When they returned, they saw nurses helping Brooke into a wheelchair.

"Good heavens," Ginger exclaimed, hurrying to her. "You, too?"

Brooke grinned, taking it all in stride. "My water just broke, so I guess she's coming early. They're admitting me now. I texted Chip, but his engine is away from the station."

Ginger hugged her. "Don't worry, we'll reach him, too." While the staff whisked Brooke away and tended to Kai, Ginger embraced Marina. "Looks like we'll welcome two babies into the family today. We've done this before, haven't we?"

Marina smiled and hugged her. "Only this time, they're not twins."

A FEW WEEKS LATER, a joyful atmosphere filled Ginger's cottage as the family gathered to celebrate the newborn cousins. Ginger's heart was full of love as she surveyed her growing family.

Sitting beside her on the sofa, Oliver tucked his hand into hers. "Happy?"

"Infinitely," she replied, squeezing his hand. "I'm happy you're here. I don't know what we would have done without you at the hospital. Locating Axe and Chip, keeping them calm, bringing food to everyone. You were wonderful."

A smile shimmered on his face. "It was a privilege being part of it all. And being part of your extraordinary life."

Ginger looked at him, struck by how excited he looked. "You look like you have a huge secret."

"Maybe I do," he said with a chuckle.

In the kitchen, Marina, Heather, and Blake organized food for everyone and set up a buffet on the dining room table. They served the new mothers first.

Kai sat in a rocking chair, cradling her newborn daughter, Stella, with Axe hovering proudly. "Our precious little star," she cooed, her face alight with happiness.

Brooke's infant, Clover, slept peacefully in her father's arms next to her. Boisterous laughter sounded outside, where their boys were tossing a ball with Leo and Scout, safely away from the water's edge.

Jack had stepped out to take a phone call some time ago.

The rear door creaked, and he returned, his face lit with a grin. "I have some incredible news," he announced, seeking out Ginger.

Crossing the room, Jack knelt in front of her. "After you approved the manuscript, I sent a draft to my agent."

"How exciting." Ginger thought Jack had done an exceptionally fine job, but she knew publishers often passed on a good manuscript, even if the agent liked it. She hoped he wouldn't be disappointed after all the work he'd put into the project. "Does she think it will sell?"

Jack's eyes twinkled. "It already did. *Decoding a Remarkable Life* sold in a huge preemptive deal with a major publisher. Film producers are also bidding on the story."

A wave of relief coursed through her, and cheers erupted in the room.

Beaming with pride, Oliver kissed her cheek.

"There's more," Jack said. "The publicist asked if you would be available for media interviews and speeches."

She was pleasantly surprised at that, if a little taken aback. "But you're the one who wrote the book."

"You're the star of it, though." Jack chuckled, rubbing the back of his neck. "They want you to do book signings and television appearances. They're particularly interested in having you speak to women about math and technology careers."

"I'm hardly an expert on that today." Ginger and Oliver exchanged a glance. "But I'll see what I can do. Our schedule is already filling up for next year."

Jack nodded. "I told her your appearances would probably be limited, and possibly to academic or research venues or children's education. Whatever you offer, they'll be happy with. I'll carry the rest of the load."

Ginger considered that. "If my words can inspire youngsters or raise funds for scholarships, I'll be honored to do what I can." She paused, gazing at the faces she loved surrounding her. "But those I wanted to inspire most are here in this room. That's why I agreed to the project."

"You won't have to travel alone," Oliver said, putting his arm around her shoulder. "If you want, I'll go with you."

"I'd like that very much." She looked forward to traveling with him this spring. Their first trip would be to Paris.

As the celebration continued, Ginger reflected on the journey of her life—the challenges she'd faced, the secrets she'd kept, and the love she'd lost and found again.

She thought of her work during the Cold War, the thrill of cracking codes, and the weight of the responsibility. She recalled the joy of raising Sandi, the pain of losing her, and the unexpected opportunity to finish raising her grand-daughters.

Her gaze swept across the room, taking in the faces of her family: Marina, Kai, and Brooke, all talented, compassionate women; their husbands and children; Heather, on the cusp of her adventures; and Oliver, her unexpected companion in this new chapter of life.

She sighed with pleasure. Hers was a life well lived, indeed. And yet, as she contemplated speeches and engagements to come, Ginger realized her story was far from over.

As if reading her thoughts, Oliver leaned in. "Ready for what comes next?" he whispered.

"More than ready," she replied. "In my mind, the best is always yet to come."

"You have no idea." Smiling broadly, Oliver kissed her hand. His eyes twinkled as if he was bursting to share a secret.

She was still basking in the glow of this happy news when Jack cleared his throat again. Like Oliver, he had an oddly mischievous glint in his eye. She wondered what they were up to now.

"That's not quite all, Ginger. Oliver has another surprise for you." Jack stepped aside to let the other man speak.

Oliver took her hand with a proud, loving expression on his face. "After certain people realized the extent of your contributions to our country and to peace among nations, you were nominated for a presidential medal. Not only that, but you've been chosen to receive one."

Realizing the magnitude of this honor, Ginger opened her mouth in surprise. "I hardly know what to say."

Oliver's smile widened. "You've been invited to Washington, D.C., to attend a special event with other awardees. You can see many of your old friends and colleagues."

The cottage erupted in cheers and congratulations, and Ginger was nearly overcome. "I'm deeply honored. But surely there are others more deserving."

Jack smiled at that. "You made important discoveries, and people want to recognize your efforts, even if it's long overdue. You will be an inspiration to others." He dipped his head. "Thank you for trusting me to write your story and shine a light on your remarkable life."

Marina, Kai, and Brooke gathered around her, peppering her with kisses and hugs. At the center of it all, Ginger laughed. "You three are my real accomplishments —you and the wonderful family you've brought me. How can I ever thank you for that?"

"Wow, what a year you've had," Kai said happily. "A biography, an award, and even a new love. Not to mention two of the cutest new babies, right?"

Oliver kissed Ginger, and Marina winked at them. Ginger reached out to her, bringing her close. "We have such a sweet life in Summer Beach."

"This is where we belong," Marina said. "With you and with each other."

"I love you all." Ginger opened her arms wide, embracing her granddaughters. "And I wish every one of you a wonderful, remarkable life."

THANK you for reading *Coral Memories* and the Coral Cottage series. Would you like a *Coral Memories* ebook bonus scene? Get it here: JanMoran.com/CoralMemories-BonusScene

If you're reading a paperback, you can download and print the PDF.

Be sure to visit Jan's online Readers Club to keep up with new books and specials, including *A Very Coral Christmas*, and the Crown Island Series. Join her Facebook Reader Club, too. And read on for Marina's delicious Quiche Lorraine Recipe.

# AUTHOR'S NOTE

More to Enjoy

If this is your first book in the Coral Cottage series, be sure to meet Marina when she first arrives in Summer Beach in *Coral Cottage*. If you haven't read the Seabreeze Inn at Summer Beach series, I invite you to meet art teacher Ivy Bay and her sister Shelly as they renovate a historic beach house in *Seabreeze Inn*, the first in the original Summer Beach series.

You might also enjoy more sunshine and international travel with a group of best friends in a series sprinkled with sunshine and second chances, beginning with *Flawless* and an exciting trip to Paris.

Finally, I invite you to read my standalone historical novels, including *Hepburn's Necklace* and *The Chocolatier*, a pair of 1950s sagas set in gorgeous Italy.

Most of my books are available in ebook, paperback or hardcover, audiobooks, and large print on my shop and from all major retailers. And as always, I wish you happy reading!

# QUICHE LORRAINE RECIPE

In *Coral Memories*, Marina makes dinner quiche for her family, adding soup, a green salad, and sweet potato fries. Easy yet elegant in its rich simplicity, a quiche Lorraine is elevated comfort food. Prepare it for breakfast, lunch, or dinner—make it ahead or serve it from the oven.

Quiche Lorraine is a light, flavorful dish I often enjoy in the summer. The custard consistency is satisfying but not heavy, so you can enjoy a walk or a swim afterward. If you're looking for low-carb keto meals, this recipe can be prepared without crust.

For a shortcut, use a ready-made pie crust or puff pastry sheets. If using puff pastry, simply lay it with the parchment paper side down in the pan and pinch sides to adhere. Don't trim the paper; this will help you lift it out of the mold after baking (let it cool a little to firm up).

The classic quiche Lorraine uses smoked bacon instead of fried bacon. Depending on what is available, use either smoked or fried bacon. If you prefer a lighter dish, use whole milk instead of heavy cream.

Quiche Lorraine originated in the Lorraine region of northeastern France centuries ago. This savory tart evolved from humble roots to culinary icon status. Initially, the quiche was a simple creation of leftover bread dough, eggs, and cream. Over time, smoked lardons (smoked bacon bits) were added, resulting in the rich, flavorful dish we know today.

Extras: The traditional French quiche Lorraine is made without cheese, but if you want to experiment with different quiche flavors, see below for variations to this recipe (just don't call it quiche Lorraine). Popular cheese additions are Gruyère, Emmenthal, or Parmesan. Add 1/2 cup grated cheese to the egg mixture (or to taste). If you would like to add chopped onions, sauté before adding to the mixture (for example, with bacon, if uncooked).

**Ingredients:**

For the pastry:

1 1/4 cups (150g) all-purpose flour
Pinch of kosher salt
4 oz. (1 stick or 8 tablespoons) (100g) cold unsalted butter, diced
2-3 tablespoons ice water (more as needed)

For the filling:

1/2 cup or 4 oz (100g) smoked bacon bits (about 3 strips diced bacon, or lardons)
4 large eggs
1 cup (200g) heavy cream (or whole milk or half-and-half)
Pinch of kosher salt
Pinch of white pepper
Pinch of nutmeg

**Pastry Instructions:**

1. Preheat oven to 350°F (180°C). For the pastry, mix flour and salt in a bowl. Cut in cold butter until mixture resembles coarse meal. Add ice water, 1 tablespoon at a time, until dough comes together. Form into a disk, wrap in plastic, and chill for 1 hour.

2. Roll out dough and drape it into a 9-inch (23cm) tart pan, mold with high sides, or pie pan. Prick bottom with a fork and chill for 30 minutes.

3. Add pie weights and bake for 10 minutes. Remove weights. Bake for 5 more minutes until lightly golden.

**Filling Instructions:**

1. Preheat oven to 350°F (180°C). Sprinkle smoked bacon over the pastry. (If using uncooked bacon or lardons, sauté first in a skillet. Drain on paper towels.)

2. Whisk together eggs, cream, pepper, salt, and nutmeg. Salt is not necessary if using smoked bacon. If adding cheese (or other ingredient variations), add it to this mixture.

3. Pour the egg mixture over the bacon in the tart pan.

4. Bake for 30-35 minutes until golden and set. Let cool for 5-10 minutes before serving.

Enjoy a slice of this creamy, savory quiche with a crisp green salad as they do in Lorraine. *Bon appétit!*

## Quiche Variations

There are several delicious variations on quiche. These variations use the basic egg and cream custard base while offering different flavor profiles and ingredients to suit various tastes and dietary preferences. Add ingredients to taste.

Cheese Quiche: Add 1/2 cup or 3 oz. (100g) grated Gruyère, Emmental, or Parmesan cheese

Caramelized Onion Quiche: Add caramelized onions for a sweeter flavor.

Salmon Quiche: Add smoked salmon instead of bacon.

Vegetarian Quiche: Replace bacon with sautéed vegetables like spinach, mushrooms, or bell peppers.

Florentine Quiche: Add spinach to the traditional recipe.

Provençale Quiche: Include cherry tomatoes, zucchini, mushroom, asparagus, or eggplant.

Ham and Cheese Quiche: Substitute ham for bacon and add Swiss or other cheese.
Broccoli and Cheddar: A popular American variation.

Crustless Quiche: For a low-carb solution, make the quiche without the pastry crust.

# ABOUT THE AUTHOR

JAN MORAN is a *USA Today* and a *Wall Street Journal* bestselling author of romantic women's fiction. A few of her favorite things include a fine cup of coffee, dark chocolate, fresh flowers, laughter, and music that touches her soul. She loves to travel, and her favorite places for inspiration are those rich with history and mystery and set against snowy mountains, palm-treed beaches, or sparkly city lights. Jan is originally from Austin, Texas, and a trace of a drawl still survives, although she has lived in Southern California near the beach for years.

Most of her books are available as audiobooks, and her historical fiction is translated into German, Italian, Polish, Dutch, Turkish, Russian, Bulgarian, Portuguese, and Lithuanian, and other languages.

If you enjoyed this book, please consider leaving a brief review online for your fellow readers where you purchased this book or on Goodreads or Bookbub.

To read Jan's other historical and contemporary novels, visit JanMoran.com. Join her VIP Readers Club mailing list and Facebook Readers Group to learn of new releases, sales and contests.

Made in United States
North Haven, CT
02 September 2024

56832930R00139